Uneasy Lies the Head

DAVID FIELD

CONTENTS

UNEASY LIES THE HEAD

Chapter One

The two men squared up to each other, eyes blazing with hatred, and each armed with a sword. The one in the blue tunic made a feint to the left, only to have his blade blocked by that wielded by the man in red. He gave a hiss of contempt and lunged forward, but his opponent in this fight to the death leaped backwards with the sure-footed stealth of a cat on a tiled roof and laughed with scorn at this feeble thrust. The blue tunic came forward again as its wearer made an unwise return lunge with his weapon that invited his opponent to knock it from his hand with an angry sideways chop. As the sword skidded across the wooden platform, the victor in the red tunic gave a shout of triumph and ran his blade unerringly through the blue garment and into the heart of the man who had been foolhardy enough to challenge him.

The vanquished duellist fell as his legs buckled beneath him, and those who had been watching expressed their appreciation with chatter, whistles, profanities and cascades of orange peel. As the noise subsided, and some began to drift away, an old man with a white beard, dressed in a gold floor-length garment with a matching crown, stepped from behind the action and addressed the remainder.

'Thus does Good overcome Evil, and here lies he who would have ravished the fair Eleanor. And so, kind friends and neighbours, be comforted in your good ways, and know that the virtuous maiden shall wed her hero, free at last of the lascivious attentions of the wicked Pantheus, Lord of Misrule. Pray thank our worthy players for their skill and devotion to the muse'.

This was the signal for the corpse in the blue tunic to scramble to his feet and join the man who had slain him in full view of a hundred paying spectators as they took their final bow. They were joined by a young woman who had not taken the trouble to lift her bodice back into place since her near ruin at the hands of the now dead Pantheus, and whose naked breasts were the main reason why most of the audience had remained to cheer the players to the echo. It was another risk they were taking, because the part she was playing ought, by law, to have been played by a boy. But Oliver Wade wrote the plays as well as appearing in most of them, and he knew what the paying public wanted to see, lawful or otherwise.

Above the catcalls and obscene invitations came a sharp call of command, and into the undercroft beneath the main room of The Cardinal Inn, on the south side of Shoreditch's Curtain Road, strode six armed men dressed in the unmistakable livery of the Tower. The crowd scattered like straw in a gale as the men were led resolutely by their commander to the edge of the wooden platform that served as a stage. He surveyed the motley crew a few feet above him, then demanded to know

'Which among you is Master Oliver Wade?'

'I am he,' admitted the tall young man with the unshaven dark stubble, dressed in the red tunic that denoted his victory in the recent stage fight, whose reincarnated victim in the blue tunic was whispering to the unravished heroine to 'hide your duckies' as he made a determined effort to pull her bodice back into place.

'Oliver Wade, you are taken up on serious charges of public lewdness,' the man announced, but the object of this announcement grinned back carelessly.

'My acting has often been described as poor – sometimes even as dire – but never have I heard it classed as "lewd". I would run you through with this sword, were it even capable of cutting through curds. All that you may have witnessed was mere pretence. Play-acting for the entertainment of the eager audience. All make believe, I assure you.'

'Her titties aren't make-believe,' a man immediately behind the leader observed with a leer as he nodded to the girl standing next to the actor in blue, who finally took his advice and fastened her bodice.

'Come with us,' the leader commanded Oliver Wade, who shook his head in amusement, far from overawed, since the Tower was one thing and the Lord Chamberlain's bloodhounds another. 'Should you and your companions be seeking a full performance, we shall be here again on the morrow, when St Leonard's great bell strikes the noonday.' There was a light snigger from one of the small company of actors ranged behind him, and the man in charge had heard enough.

'The rest of your band of idle and insolent vagabonds may well choose to risk another visitation on the morrow, but for today my orders are only to take you in charge and convey you to Newgate.'

'On whose authority?' Oliver challenged him. 'The City Fathers who control what is staged in their bailiwick have no jurisdiction outside London's walls, which is why so many of my calling pursue their trade here in Shoreditch, or across the river in Southwark.' The man's face darkened.

'I come here not to pander to the twitterings of the Aldermen of the City, but to enforce the will of the Lord Chamberlain.'

'The Master of the Royal Revels?' Oliver enquired with an insolent raising of the eyebrows. 'Since the death of Her

Majesty – God rest her soul – there has surely been no need for that worthy dignitary to seek out fresh masques for the royal banqueting halls. And indeed, I had no idea that we were so well regarded.'

'Enough of your insolence!' the official bellowed as he turned to the two men immediately behind him. 'Take him up, and if he resists you may run him through.'

There were gasps of fear from his fellow actors, but Oliver raised a reassuring hand.

'Fear not, he is bluffing. I know defeat when I see it in the eyes of another man, and this man who claims to be a mouthpiece for the Lord Chamberlain wears Tower livery, and knows full well that Tower bullies possess no authority to arrest by force of arms on Lord Chamberlain's business.'

'Perhaps not the Lord Chamberlain,' the leader of the armed group smirked back mockingly, 'but his was not the order I received. My instruction came in person from Master Secretary Cecil, who has long demonstrated his authority to remove the head of whomsoever threatens the peace of the realm.'

'I was not aware that our performances were so loud,' Oliver jested back as he made a great show of laying his pretend sword down on the wooden boards of the somewhat rustic stage, jumped down and held out his arms for them to be tied at the wrists.

'Lead on, good sir,' he smiled jocularly at his captor. 'I wish to make Newgate in time for a hearty supper.'

There was no supper, hearty or otherwise. Nor was there any breakfast or dinner the following day, but at least Oliver appeared to have been granted the luxury of a cell to himself, he consoled himself as he listened to the yells, screams, and protestations of injustice that echoed up and down the dank corridors with their low stone ceilings. The all-pervading smell of the place was almost overpoweringly that of human fear and degradation, and the solitude was just becoming a discomfort when the door to his five feet square charnel house ground open, and a squat figure was ushered through it with much bowing and scraping.

Oliver peered up at him in the dim light that diffused the cell through the holes in its brickwork, but made no effort to rise from his seated position on the bare earth in the angle of two walls. His visitor was almost a midget, and most certainly not blessed with that sturdiness of frame required to play the romantic hero in those plays that Oliver had recently taken to writing for his own band of players. As if Dame Nature had not cursed the man enough, he was also obliged to stand at a somewhat absurd angle, given a congenital curvature of the spine, and as a final kick he had clearly only survived smallpox at the cost of a pockmarked countenance that the straggly beard did nothing to conceal. He glared down at Oliver where he sat with an amused grin. There was a lengthy silence, at the end of which Oliver was the first to speak.

'You have come to share my solitude? What be your crime? Clearly not that of pickpocket, to judge by the richness of your attire. Silk, if I assess aright?'

'I am your gaoler, you impudent wretch!' the man replied with a disdainful sneer.

'You are hardly dressed for the part,' Oliver observed drily, and the sneer deepened as his visitor announced 'I am Sir Robert Cecil, Secretary of State to the former Queen Elizabeth.'

'Who departed this life some days ago,' Oliver reminded him. 'They say that Elizabeth died without leaving any heir, which presumably means that you now serve no-one in your former office. So now you are reduced to earning your living by imprisoning the innocent?'

'You are guilty of the vilest lewdness – you and your band of dissolute and blasphemous vagabonds. You parade shameless whores in a state of undress for the ungodly to leer at in exchange for their few pence. You also operate without a patron, unlike the more respectable of theatre companies. But I am not here to chastise your bawdy choice of employment.'

'But before we leave that matter unchallenged,' Oliver replied, 'you should be advised that in my theatre we prefer to depict life as it really is, and not smooth it over with the daub of respectability. As for the nakedness of the Lady Eleanor in my latest play, would she have been more convincing had she emerged from a vicious attack upon her virtue with all her garments intact? Fie, sir, you have no sense of drama.'

'She should not have been in your company in the first place,' Cecil fired back. 'It is the law that women in the theatre should be portrayed by young boys, as you must be well aware. And yet I am advised by those who took you up that there was a whore in your company displaying her duckies in the lewdest manner.' Oliver snorted.

'And what could be more lewd than pretty boys dressing up in women's clothing, and parading themselves around in public?'

'Enough!' Cecil commanded, before looking round the confined space with a frown.

'I see that there is no place to sit other than in the dust in which your arse is currently located, and it pains me to remain standing for any undue length of time, so let us proceed to our main business. You were once a fine soldier, were you not?'

'I was a soldier, certainly,' Oliver conceded with a darkened face. 'In the service of my Lord of Essex, in Ireland. If you are truly who you say you are, then as I heard it you were no more a friend of Robert Devereux than was I.'

'Is that why you deserted his service?'

'I did *not* desert!' Oliver yelled back angrily. 'I sought a discharge from his service, certainly, due to his promotion of favourites whose lack of military prowess endangered all our lives, not to mention the brutality that he visited on simple peasant families. It was little wonder that his mission failed.'

'You have proof that he granted you your discharge?' Cecil smiled maliciously. 'For if not you are a deserter, and in these uncertain times that could be deemed treason.'

'As for proof,' Oliver glowered back up at him, 'I could once have called him to witness. However, since you were instrumental in securing his execution for the same crime of which you now seem anxious to accuse me, I can no longer call upon him to prove my innocence. Fortunately I had the presence of mind to secure my honourable discharge in writing, and it is at my lodgings, where it remains safe from sneak thieves who would have no use for it anyway.'

'Your pestilential room above the cats-meat shop in Hog Lane?' Cecil sneered. 'While you have been confined in here, I have taken the opportunity to have your pigsty searched, and you may rest assured that it no longer contains the proof of your discharge.'

'You stole it?' Oliver demanded, outraged and horror-stricken as he suddenly realised the peril that this theft placed him in, and was little encouraged by Cecil's continuing leer.

'By whatever means it has become lost, you are no longer able to prove that you did not desert the late Queen's service. This exposes you to a charge of treason. How that will grieve your dear father!'

'Leave him out of this discourse, and tell me what it is you require of me!' Oliver retorted angrily, resisting the temptation to leap to his feet and shake the life out of the despicable but dangerous little pygmy. But Cecil was enjoying the moment.

'Your father would be utterly destroyed by shame and grief, would he not? He has a record of military service under the Crown even more laudable than yours, and he currently has hopes of a knighthood and appointment to the honourable – and profitable – post of Lieutenant of the Tower. How would he feel to learn that his only son - even one from whom he is estranged - had been hung, drawn and quartered on Tower Hill for the amusement of the malodorous mob? Your final act upon the stage of life?'

'For aught I know, he would not grieve,' Oliver replied sourly. 'We are at odds, as you must know, since I abandoned the soldier's life and took instead to the theatre.'

'But he still provides you with the meagre allowance that keeps your body from starvation?' Cecil reminded him. 'And whether he loves you or no, the disgrace of your departure from this world would be sufficient to destroy his ambition for future advancement, would it not?'

'I am probably not the first to advise you that you are a double-died bastard,' Oliver growled, 'so let us dispense with my opinion of you, and tell me what it is that you seek from me.'

'Both your sword arm and your ability to pose as that which you are not. You may call it 'acting' if you must, but for me it will be a valuable addition to your martial talents.'

'In what capacity?' Oliver enquired coldly. 'Do you seek to employ me in the same devious games that led the Queen's favourite to the block, and by all accounts occasioned her death from the grief of it?'

'You presume too highly,' Cecil smiled back confidently. 'I can call upon the services of others more qualified and talented than yourself – men trained by the late Sir Francis Walsingham, my late father's right hand man in devious subterfuge. He also taught me, but I have higher matters to which I must attend, and I must therefore take my leave, having, as I understand it, secured your services as well.'

'You go to plot the downfall of others?' Oliver enquired as he rose to his feet and dusted off the stage costume in which he was still attired. Cecil's smile broadened.

'To the contrary, I go to welcome into the kingdom its next King. He will hopefully be grateful that I have been able to secure him a second crown to go with his first in Scotland. He will also, no doubt, be doubly grateful to learn that I can assure him of continued peace within his new realm, towards which peace you will in due course play your part. You are free to leave this shithole, and return to your own shithole. You will be contacted in due course. Please ensure that you are available when that happens, for you are too useful to me to have your entrails removed at this early stage in our relationship.'

***

It was a much less arrogant and triumphant Cecil who bowed his hunched back as low as his spine would allow as he halted a few paces away from the ornate chair in which sat the man for whose future fortunes he had striven, and who would no doubt suitably reward him in time to come.

That man was James Stuart, James VI of Scotland, and the son of the Mary Stuart who had been executed on the reluctant, and some said unknowing, order of Queen Elizabeth some years in the past. He had ruled Scotland, first under a succession of regents, and then in his own right, and he was now in his mid thirties, with very pronounced views on certain matters of religion and kingship.

Elizabeth had been dead for only eight days, but on the very day of her death James had been proclaimed King of England in a form of words drafted by Robert Cecil, with whom James had been in regular communication throughout those dreary weeks in which 'Gloriana's' life had been ebbing away. It had been Cecil who had emerged from the death chamber with the insistence that Elizabeth had indicated her preference for James as her successor rather than one of the more shadowy rival claimants, and given the power vacuum from which the nation suffered at that time, and Cecil's stranglehold over what passed for a Council of State during those dying days, no-one had dared to argue with him. Cecil was now in attendance on the new monarch as he approached London for a triumphant entrance organised by the man who knelt before him, head bowed, but his brain alive with expectation.

'You keep a fine house here at Theobalds,' James advised Cecil with a broad smile that masked his astonishment that someone so uncomely and deformed could exercise such authority in his new realm. 'I would perhaps wish to purchase it from you, since it is so conveniently situated for London.' He spoke with the heavy accent that betrayed his erstwhile life north of the border that had been hotly contested for centuries between the two nations that were now about to become combined under one crown. It was the first time that the two men had met face to face, and Cecil was slightly taken aback by the way that his new monarch pronounced his words.

'It would be my pleasure and privilege to convey same to Your Majesty,' was all that Cecil could manage by way of reply as he racked his brain for ways of introducing those matters of which he wished James to become aware. But James was ahead of him.

'I must thank you in person for all that you have done to ensure that the crown of England was passed to he who was most qualified to receive it,' James lisped in his quaint way that others often mistook for effeminacy. 'Now tell me, is it a crown that sits easily on the head of its rightful claimant?'

'Most assuredly, Your Majesty,' Cecil glowed as James waved his hand in a signal for him to rise and take the seat next to his, which was so large and ornate that the little Courtier was almost lost to view inside it. 'But I must advise you that it is heavily in debt, due to the mismanagement of those who came before me.'

'One of whom was your own father, yes?' James teased him with a look of mild amusement on his long face. Cecil smiled back reassuringly with a prepared answer.

'Not him, Your Majesty. It was he who advised your revered cousin Elizabeth so well that she was able to send the Armada fleeing back to Spain. But those who followed him were less worthy of the peace that he had secured for England, and I speak principally of the Earl of Essex, who sought to line his pockets from being the late Queen's favourite. Fortunately I was able to reveal his treachery, and he paid the price on the block. But as a result our navy is all but disbanded, while our army is effectively non-existent, and the Treasury is much depleted.'

'I would seek a peace with Spain as my first priority,' James replied in a tone of voice that left little invitation for argument. 'With peace between our two nations we should have little need for any army or navy.'

Cecil felt the words choking in his throat, but James had to be properly advised. 'There may be a difficulty with that, Your Majesty.'

James raised his eyebrows in challenge. 'And what might that be?' he enquired.

'Catholics, Your Majesty,' Cecil replied, comfortable in the knowledge that James was a confirmed Protestant. 'They pose a threat even yet, despite all her late Majesty's pious determination to keep England free from the pernicious influence of Rome. You may be aware that my mentor in matters of national security, Sir Francis Walsingham, was most successful in smoking out Jesuits wherever they crept into the nation, but that has not deterred many of the minor nobles in the land from fomenting for greater tolerance of their blasphemous practices.'

'And the more senior nobles?' James enquired with a look of apprehension bordering upon annoyance. Cecil lowered his glance to what he hoped was an appropriate angle of humility before replying.

'I have taken the liberty, in the confident knowledge that

you would approve same, of recruiting those who are well qualified, both by experience and loyalty to your person, to seek out those who may be planning to clamour for greater religious freedom. As at present known, there appear to be none within your loyal Council who would seek to ally with them. They are staunch Protestants to a man, and would give no heed to any such noisome clamouring. But neither should you be seen to persecute those misguided disciples of the Bishop of Rome, if you seek a lasting peace with Spain.'

James sat deep in thought for a moment, then looked enquiringly back at Cecil.

'Would it not bode well for any approach to Philip of Spain were I to treat Catholics more kindly?' he enquired. 'It was my cousin Elizabeth's belief that all men should be free to worship as their conscience dictates, was it not?'

'Indeed it was, in her early years,' Cecil conceded, 'but they proved so ungrateful as to plot against her life and continued reign. There were many intrigues, particularly in her later years, and some were so base as to name your dear late mother as their muse and inspiration.'

'I need not be reminded of that rank injustice,' James snapped back, and Cecil chose a change of tack.

'My point entirely, Your Majesty. These Catholics will stoop as low as is necessary for the right to openly pursue their blasphemies, and it falls to us to ensure that they do not succeed as well as they did in former years. There is also the matter of your Council.'

'Which you control, do you not?' James enquired, and Cecil lowered his gaze even more. 'Indeed, I am privileged to be in a position to convene that Council, your Majesty, in my prior capacity as Secretary of State. But with a change of monarch comes the opportunity for change, and . . . '

'I wish no change in that regard,' James hastily confirmed as he interrupted Cecil. 'You will be content to serve me as you once served my cousin?'

'With a grateful heart, Your Majesty,' Cecil smiled as he looked back up and breathed a long sigh of relief. 'And you may rely on me to ensure that your Council does not prove too troublesome to you, as indeed they might, were you to be seen to allow any more laxity to Catholics.'

'And why should I concern myself over what the Council thinks?' James enquired with irritation. Cecil failed to hear the warning in the words, and blundered on.

'Because you will require their approval for the most important matters of State, Your Majesty.'

He became aware of his error as James's eyes flashed angrily.

'I am the King of England, Cecil – and England will obey my will, are we understood?'

Cecil had barely nodded his concession when James continued in heated tones.

'I have been appointed by God, and to God only am I answerable, you miserable little man! Do not presume to tell me that my will must be filtered through an assembly of little men like yourself, whom God has rejected in His choice of King. I will employ you to ensure that my will is implemented, but I will not go before this so-called Council like some errant schoolboy offering up his Greek Grammar to be corrected. Do we understand each other?'

'Completely, Your Majesty,' Cecil whispered back, both terrified and appalled in equal measure.

'This is as well, since your continued office will depend

upon it,' James replied as his face broke into a smile. 'But thus far, I am satisfied that I am well served. See to it that the Catholic question does not need to be raised again in my hearing. And now give me tidings of my proposed triumphant progress into London on the morrow. Have you engaged enough musicians, think you?'

Oliver Wade stretched his arms and legs as he descended into the morning sunlight down the steps that led from his squalid apartment on the second floor into the bustling street with shops along its length. His first stop as usual was the baker's stall two doors down, where the buxom wife of the elderly proprietor stood proudly behind their assortment of fresh loaves, calling out to those who hurried by about their lawful business. She smiled as Oliver walked over, kissed her warmly on the mouth, pinched her bottom with his right hand and stole his daily loaf with the other. He turned on his heel and walked smartly back up Hog Lane, intending to make an early breakfast of the two day old cheese that was beginning to ripen in a way that Nature had never intended, washed down with the remains of the wine stolen from the cellar of The Cardinal the previous day. Then he became aware of the two armed men guarding the foot of his outside staircase.

'Oliver Wade?' one of them enquired, and Oliver nodded. 'Secretary Cecil requires to speak with you,' he was advised.

'So soon?' Oliver replied in what was more a statement of annoyance than a question. 'Had he given me more warning, I would have ensured that my lodgings were more suitable to host such a worthy noble.'

'Not here, you bumblefuck,' the other man replied less politely. 'We are instructed to convey you to Whitehall. You may bring your breakfast with you.'

Chapter Two

Cecil allowed himself a superior smile as Oliver was ushered into his inner chamber, his loaf of bread still under his arm and a resigned expression on his face.

'You will find, Master Wade,' Cecil sneered, 'that here at Whitehall we are fed at royal expense. I can supply you with a *lettre de bouche* that will entitle you to eat thrice daily in the Buttery on the lower floor, where all menials are wont to take their meals. There was no need to come accompanied by your dinner.'

'It was meant to be my breakfast,' Oliver grumbled, 'until your oafs escorted me down here like some common criminal. My dinner will hopefully be taken at The Cardinal, after we stage our next performance of "The Salvation of Lady Eleanor". Or do you have other calls on my time?'

'Take that seat, and listen carefully to what I have to say,' Cecil commanded, and Oliver duly obliged. Cecil lowered his voice so as to be barely audible above the busy hum of the clerks in the outer chamber.

'We have a new King, as you are no doubt aware. He is from Scotland, and he knows little of our ways. He also has a strange notion that he can rule without Council, which presents me with certain difficulties, but also certain freedoms. In particular he wishes to rule without the constant need to either consult or be consulted, and he has entrusted me with ensuring that nothing occurs within the realm that either requires his grudging attention or demands the consent of Council. A Council for which, it would seem, he has scant regard.'

'So you have effectively become our new King?' Oliver enquired with a deprecating smile, which Cecil extinguished with a stern glare. 'This is not a matter for levity, Master Wade, as you will shortly discover. But before that, would I be correct in my understanding that you are of the Protestant persuasion?'

'If I were a Catholic, I would hardly disclose that fact to you,' Oliver replied with one of his insubordinate grins, and Cecil nodded.

'Quite so. And your opinion of Catholics?'

'Like bed bugs,' Oliver replied. 'Irritating in the extreme, but of no immediate hazard to one's health.'

'And in that you would be fatally misled,' Cecil frowned. 'Almost all the threats to the Crown that have been posed since I first learned my trade under my highly regarded father have come from disaffected Catholics who seek to invite the Bishop of Rome back into our forms of worship.'

Oliver paused in thought before adding his contribution. 'I recall the execution of the Scottish Queen some years ago, although I was a mere boy at the time. My father, however, was one of those who was enlisted at Tilbury when the Spanish King sought his revenge.'

'It was *my* father who organised the naval force that sent the Spaniards packing,' Cecil replied gloatingly, 'but you clearly remember sufficient for me to explain to you why the Catholic threat remains, and why I must take steps to suppress it before it comes to the King's ears, and invokes his ire at having to put aside his main pleasures in order to deal with it, and perhaps become beholden to his Council in its suppression.'

'If the Spanish have abandoned their ambitions for England, from whence comes this renewed threat?' Oliver enquired, and Cecil smiled unpleasantly. 'You may forget the Spanish for the time, since the threat comes from much closer to home than that. Indeed, our newly installed King James is mindful of making a formal peace treaty with Spain, in the naive belief that this will put an end to any challenge to his throne from those with Catholic inclinations. Regrettably, that is far from being the reality of the situation, but I for one would hesitate to incur his wrath by being so unwise as to argue with him.'

'So it is your intention to deal with this Catholic threat from within without recourse to his Majesty?'

'Precisely. But not alone. You may perhaps begin to perceive why I might need some assistance from those who can work my counter intrigues without exciting attention.'

'And you number me among these worker ants?' Oliver enquired, as if he had not already deduced that. 'I do indeed,' Cecil replied with an ingratiating smile. 'As I have already advised you, the combination of your undoubted skills with a sword and your boasted talents as a vulgar theatrical player will be of particular assistance in all this.'

'And I think that we have already discussed the price of my refusal,' Oliver muttered, to an even broader smile from Cecil. 'Indeed we have. A final farewell performance on Tower Hill. Now, to your first task. Are you familiar with a place called "The Clink"?'

Oliver grinned. 'Thank God I am not, although I have been threatened with it more than once. It's a prison of sorts, is it not?'

'It is indeed,' Cecil confirmed. 'It is located across the river in Southwark, convenient for others of your misguided trade who have begun to build theatres outside the effective control of the City Aldermen. It is under the management of the Bishop of Winchester, and in the main it is reserved for blasphemers, although of late it has also housed plotters against the true faith, if that is not the same thing.'

'And why do you acquaint me with this information?' Oliver enquired guardedly. 'Is this another of your threats?' Cecil laughed, a somewhat chilling chattering noise that seemed to come from another place entirely than his throat. 'Indeed not. Rest assured that should I have occasion to imprison you, it will be in that place that your father so earnestly wishes to govern. So far as I am aware, the Clink can boast no instruments of persuasion. It is as soft a regime as could be imagined for a so-called prison, with laxities that allow prisoners to order in their own meals, to acquire whores for their bodily comfort, and to receive visitors. Those who call themselves gaolers are little better than stewards attending to the needs of their imprisoned masters, and are easily bribed.'

'By you, presumably? Oliver enquired, and Cecil nodded.

'Indeed by me, and it is by such means that I am advised of a regular visitor to a certain prisoner, whose name is William Watson. This visitor is a woman who chooses to assume the guise of a whore, but given that the man who she visits is a Catholic priest, it is suspected – by me, primarily – that she is conveying messages back and forth between this Watson and others who may be planning to bring pressure on our new King to grant greater concessions to those of their misguided faith.'

'Pressure of what ilk?' Oliver enquired, only to be met by

a stern frown from Cecil. 'That is for you to determine. I merely point you in the direction of what may prove to be a Catholic plot in its early stages. Watson took the trouble to travel to Scotland while our first King James was on its throne as the sixth of that name. He pledged the support of a group of Catholics, of which he claimed to be the spokesman, for James's claim to the throne left by Elizabeth, during those months when it was well known that she was approaching death. In return, he was seeking greater indulgence towards those of his shared faith, of which as yet there has been little sign. Certainly his Majesty has made no mention of it in my hearing, and it is my informed guess that this man Watson is engaged in a scheme designed to reinforce his demands. He is known to be opposed in this by a band of unashamed Jesuits, who fear that any open rebellion will worsen the position of Catholics in England, and who are resting their hopes on Philip of Spain demanding greater tolerance as a condition of the peace treaty that King James is pursuing with him.'

Oliver shook his head, as if seeking to throw water off his unruly black locks. 'This is a great deal for me to absorb in one sitting, and I am due back at my theatre shortly.'

'You will leave here when I say that you may!' Cecil advised him sharply, 'and that will not be until you have satisfied me that you at least comprehend the simple role in all this that I have allocated to you.'

Oliver smiled back reassuringly. 'You wish me to ascertain who this lady might be who is visiting this man Watson, and on whose behalf she makes these visits?'

'That is correct,' Cecil confirmed, only mildly reassured. 'The gaoler who is in my pay is called John Dugger, and you are to seek him out and tell him that you are sent by "Thomas Grange", which is the name he knows me by. He believes me to be a servant of Treasurer Sackville, a prominent Protestant and favoured Councillor of the late Queen Elizabeth, and I would be obliged if you say nothing to disabuse him of this subterfuge, in case these enquiries blow up in our faces. You will give him ten marks for all he can tell you regarding this mysterious woman visitor who Watson receives weekly, and it is in this bag, along with a further ten marks for any expenses that you may incur in the course of your investigations. You will report your findings to me at the earliest, and if I have not seen you back here within the week I will seek you out and have you racked in the Tower. Do you have any questions regarding any of this? If not, you may depart in order to dupe others out of the pennies they hand over in order to view your daily bawdry.'

Assuring Cecil that he had no uncertainty regarding what was expected of him, Oliver took his leave and hurried through the busy streets until he was safely through the other side of the ancient City and back into the cramped laneways of Shoreditch, where he was welcomed back by his band of players with expressions of relief.

'I had hoped to play your role, should you be delayed much longer,' Matthew Partridge pouted, and Oliver smiled encouragingly as he patted him on the shoulder. 'Thus was always the fate of the understudy,' he assured the young and keen recent addition to his band of players, 'but rest assured that the day is not long away when I shall be missing from the company, and your opportunity will come.'

***

Two afternoons later he was installed in the gaolers' room

in The Clink, handing ten marks to the evil smelling John Dugger, and absorbing some of the information he had been sent to acquire.

'She's very comely, sir, and quite the lady, which is what makes me think she's no whore. When the prisoners gets a goose to ride in their cells, we gaolers likes to spy on them through the flap in the door while they goes at it, but I never seen this one even whip out her duckies. All they seems to do is sit and talk, and what with him being one of them there Cafflick types, I thought it as well to let Master Grange know all about it, him being so generous and all.'

'You have no idea who this woman might be?' Oliver enquired as he did his best impersonation of a trusted emissary of a nobleman, but Dugger shook his head, releasing more greasy dandruff into the air between them.

'No, sir. She seems quite high-born, to judge by her manner and everything, and like I said she's proper nice to look at, but you never can tell, can you?'

'Does she visit on the same day every week?'

'Yeah – always on a Thursday. She gets here about dinner time, then sits with the prisoner for about a couple of hours or so, and like I said they doesn't do nothing like – well, you know, like going to it or nothing – and then she just ups and leaves. She always comes with a few treats for the prisoner, like cakes and things, and sometimes a flagon of wine or something, and it's always in this here blue bag. That set me thinking that perhaps there's messages or something being taken in and out, which is why I took the trouble to tell that Master Grange what you works for.'

'And you did the right thing,' Oliver assured him. 'Always on a Thursday, you said?'

'That's right, and always after dinner.'

Oliver thought for a moment, then smiled as a plan came into his mind. 'It's Tuesday today, so if I come back here the day after next, you can point her out to me?'

'Certainly can, sir. Then what will you do? Only I wouldn't want to get into trouble with the Governor here. I needs my job, see?'

'Don't worry about that for a single moment,' Oliver smiled back reassuringly as he mentally selected those who would be accompanying him when Thursday came.

***

Two days later, the lady thanked John Dugger profusely in cultured tones for his customary assistance as he closed the door to Watson's cell and accompanied her back down the corridor past his open room door, then let her out into the small courtyard. As soon as the heavy front door had closed behind her he scuttled back to his room, where Oliver sat expectantly, and had it confirmed that she was the lady in question. Oliver thanked Dugger, handed him another five marks, and slipped out through the front door in pursuit of his quarry.

He followed at a safe distance behind her as she made her way down the narrow laneway towards Bankside, where she no doubt intended to take a wherry across to the north bank of the Thames, probably to the Westminster steps, from where she could easily acquire a coach to take her home, wherever that might be. There was no urgency, since he knew that she would shortly be brought to a rude halt, although he deeply regretted having to cancel today's planned opening performance of his new play.

Right on cue, two rough looking men stepped out into the

roadway ahead of her, causing her to halt with a startled scream. Each man was armed with a cudgel, and they roughly demanded her purse. She was in the process of fumbling for it in her cloak when Oliver dashed forward, sword drawn, and in a loud voice ordered the two ruffians to make themselves scarce 'or you will taste my steel in your innards!' With squawks of fear his two actors ran off down the street, leaving Oliver to turn and enquire solicitously if she had been harmed.

'No, thanks to you,' the lady replied breathlessly. 'You are a brave man, sir, and I probably owe you my life.'

'Well, your purse at least,' Oliver replied with suitable modesty. 'There are too many of these former soldiers running amok in the streets. 'Tis a pity that our late Queen discharged so many of them without pensions when she had no further use for them. Now they are reduced to begging, or have been forced to become footpads. I am embarrassed to have been a party to their recruitment in the first place.'

'You are a soldier?' the woman enquired as she took in his tall frame and dark countenance with an approving glance. 'I was – once,' he admitted, 'but now I am obliged to make my living as a footman inside a nobleman's house on The Strand. I have just been to visit my widowed mother, who lives poorly in one of the cottages a few streets behind us. I can only pass her a few shillings from time to time, since I too am somewhat reduced in circumstances.'

The lady began to reach for her purse as she offered to reward him for his service, but he held up a hand in protest. 'Forgive me, Mistress, but I did not come to your aid in search of reward. Were I to do so, I would be no better than those ruffians who would have stolen from you.'

'But I must show my gratitude in some meaningful way,' the lady smiled. 'Would you perhaps consent to be my guest for supper this evening? I am lodging at "The White Bishop", just along the river bank here. I would be pleased to make the further acquaintance of so brave a man, and it may be that I can put you in the way of a better situation in life.'

'That would be most kind of you, Mistress,' Oliver beamed back at her, barely able to believe his good fortune. 'Shall we say around sunset?'

The sun was sinking fast downriver in the direction of Westminster as Oliver was ushered into the private dining chamber of the White Bishop, to find his hostess standing smiling in front of a blazing log fire and holding out a mug of mulled wine. Servers were hastily loading the small table with all manner of tempting dishes, and Oliver felt a slight pang of conscience over his deception. Only slight, since the lady was indeed most comely, and he was indeed most hungry.

'So might you be interested in a position in the country?' the lady enquired as they sat down and helped themselves to slices of honeyed pork and freshly baked manchet loaf. 'I'm no farmer,' Oliver grinned, but the lady shook her head as she smiled and reached out to place a cool hand on his wrist.

'I had in mind a position much like the one you currently hold,' she advised him, 'although in such a position you would be responsible for the personal safety of only one person – me. I was much impressed with your boldness and good manners earlier today, and my uncle is inclined to worry when I make these trips to London unaccompanied, in order to see to the continued welfare of his old friend William Watson.'

'You do not live in London?' Oliver enquired casually, and she shook her head. 'No, in a place called Ollerton, which is in Nottinghamshire, well to the north. I reside on the estate of my uncle Sir Griffin Markham, and have done since my father died some years ago. He was a soldier also, although he fought in Flanders under the Earl of Leicester.'

'So your name is Markham?' Oliver enquired naturally, and she nodded. 'Yes, but I would wish you to call me by my first name, which is Harriet. And what, pray, is yours?'

Oliver blushed on cue as he apologised. 'Most remiss of me. My name is Thomas – Thomas Grange. So, Harriet Markham, you travel to London to see to the welfare of a friend of your uncle?'

'Indeed,' Harriet confirmed as her gaze dropped to the board from which they were eating. 'Do not think any the less of me, I beg you, but the man to whom I refer – whose name, as I already mentioned, is William Watson – is imprisoned for his religious beliefs.'

'And what might those be? Oliver enquired disingenuously, and Harriet appeared to hesitate for a moment before responding. 'He is a Catholic.'

'And that is enough to have him imprisoned?' Oliver enquired in a tone of disbelief. Harriet nodded, observing 'I take it from that response that you are not fully aware of how matters stand with those who follow what they believe to be the true faith in this country?'

Oliver shook his head. 'I have never been a great follower of the Church in any of its forms, I have to admit. I was raised as a Protestant, and I am aware that we should be opposed to those who follow the Catholic ways, but within my heart I cannot bring myself to do so.'

'A true Christian,' Harriet murmured as she once again extended her cool hand, this time in order to take Oliver's hand in hers and give it a gentle squeeze. 'Would that there were more like you in this world. It would not offend you to learn that I share the faith of my uncle and his dear friend?'

'I would not care were you a Mohammedan,' Oliver smiled back, beginning to wonder if this pleasant evening might end with something more carnal in an upper chamber. She was certainly an alluring prospect, with silvery blonde locks cascading onto her shoulders, deep set blue eyes and what looked like a full bosom, so far as he could make out under her heavily brocaded gown. She blushed, and hastened to change the subject.

'Regarding my visits to Southwark, they are made every week, in the estate coach. It is my almost constant occupation, since even in good weather the journey takes two days in each direction, and there is the constant fear of footpads or armed robbers. The coachman is quite elderly, and I doubt his ability to fend off those such as I encountered today. I would obviously be much relieved in my mind were you to travel with me, and whatever you are being feed at present, I would be more than happy to match it – perhaps even improve on it.'

Oliver was spellbound at the prospect, almost forgetting why he was there in the first place, but was recalled to his mission by her reference to the length of the journey she undertook every week.

'Your uncle must indeed be very fond of the man in prison, if he sends his niece to enquire as to his welfare every week. Has he not offered to make the journey himself, rather than rely on a beautiful young lady such as yourself to risk her life and honour on indifferent roads?' Harriet grimaced.

'Would that the same gallant thought should come to him, but the sad fact is that he fears that should his association with Watson be revealed, he might also be imprisoned.'

'But they pose no danger to the throne,' Oliver pointed out. 'Or do they?'

Harriet's face hardened, and she withdrew her hand, almost in acknowledgement that she had spoken too freely. Her manner became more businesslike as she appeared to concentrate on peeling a plum from the fruit bowl, then enquired 'So, would you be interested in my proposition?'

'I will certainly give it the consideration it deserves,' Oliver replied as he speculated in his mind how such an arrangement would serve several purposes at once. For Cecil, the opportunity to keep a closer observation on communications between a man deemed dangerous enough to be imprisoned and his Catholic friends, and for himself the possibility of becoming more than a mere bodyguard to a beautiful lady residing on a wealthy estate.

Harriet smiled ingratiatingly and began to rise from the table. 'Join me here again for supper on the Thursday of next week, and give me your answer.' She held out her hand to be kissed, then pulled Oliver gently towards her and kissed him lightly on the lips. 'For my handsome saviour,' she murmured as she slipped past him and headed for the door, leaving Oliver both confused and aroused at the same time.

As he left the inn, greatly conflicted in his mind, he heard a church bell somewhere boom out eight times, and he hurried down the Southwark steps, handed the wherryman five marks and demanded to be transported upriver to

29

Whitehall. The tide was with them, and in a matter of minutes he was being admitted to Cecil's chambers where, thankfully, the man was taking a late supper at his desk. He put down his eating knife as Oliver was admitted, and wasted no time in small talk.

'Well?'

'Well,' Oliver gushed, 'I have achieved all that you required of me, and more. The lady is one Harriet Markham, the niece of Sir Griffin Markham, who has an estate somewhere in the vicinity of Nottingham. They are both Catholics, and she visits the prisoner Watson on Thursday of each week, making the round trip in four days, conveying information between her uncle and Watson. By a subtle subterfuge involving two of my actors I succeeded in securing her confidence to such an extent that she invited me to take supper with her at the inn at which she is lodging overnight – the "White Bishop" in Bankside - and I so far avoided any suspicion she might have entertained that she has invited me to accompany her on future journeys between her estate and The Clink, in the capacity of her bodyguard. Should I take up such a role, of course, I may pass on to you any further intelligence that I might acquire.'

'You have done well,' Cecil conceded grudgingly. 'I already knew of the connection between Watson and Markham, but was not aware that they were still in such regular communication. "The White Bishop" in Bankside, you say?'

'Yes,' Oliver confirmed eagerly. 'So am I to take up her invitation?'

'Leave it with me,' Cecil instructed him. 'I will be in touch when need be.'

The following day Oliver made his way as usual through the noisy throng of street traders, locals about their lawful business, and prostitutes lurking in doorways about their unlawful business, and entered the main room of The Cardinal to find several of his players still dressed as if for the street.

'Why are you not in costume?' he enquired of James Winters, cast as 'The Chorus', and therefore due to go on stage ahead of the remaining cast. There was an awkward silence, and it was Meg Tyler who answered.

'We weren't sure whether or not to cancel today's performance, as a mark of respect.'

'Respect for who, exactly?'

'The "Southwark Players",' she replied as tears welled in her eyes. 'Half the company died in an explosion last night. The news came across the river by the wherryman who lives in the same lodgings as me.'

Oliver's heart felt as if it had opted to descend to his stomach as the first inklings took form in his brain. 'The Southwark Players have their theatre on Bankside, do they not?' he enquired.

When Meg nodded while wiping away an escaping tear, Oliver asked his next question in a voice that to his ears had all the quality of a funeral bell. 'How did this explosion come to be caused – were they seeking to imitate a castle under siege or something?'

'No,' Meg gurgled. 'The explosion was next door, at an inn. Everyone lodged at the inn perished, and seven of the actors from next door along with them. They say that Bankside is but a pile of broken bodies.'

'The inn?' Oliver enquired hollowly. 'Does it have a name?'

'It was called "The White Bishop", seemingly,' Meg replied as she clung to Timothy Bryant's shoulder for consolation.

'You were correct in your assumption,' Oliver advised the assembled company. 'There will be no performance today.'

Like a man hoping to awake from a bad dream he wandered outside, where he stared, unseeing, at the bustle in the street, and questioned what in God's name he'd got himself involved in.

Chapter Three

'It was a wicked, wanton, evil and totally unforgivable taking of human life!' Oliver protested as he pushed his way into Cecil's office chamber through the largely token gestures of restraint from several clerks in the outer room. Cecil didn't even bother to look up from the document on the table before him as he gestured languidly with one hand for Oliver to take a seat. After pointedly taking his time over what he was reading, and initialling the foot of it, he looked back up at Oliver's face, still red with anger.

'To what are you referring?' Cecil enquired in a tone of studied indifference. Oliver was beside himself as he yelled back 'The wanton waste of human life! Or was it mere coincidence that "The White Bishop", and the theatre next door to it, were blown to Hades on the same night that I advised you that Watson's messenger was lodging there?'

'It was essential, for two reasons,' Cecil replied calmly as he replaced his quill in its holder and sat back in his chair, folding his hands on his chest in the manner of a self-satisfied clergyman. 'The first of those reasons was the more obvious one that it will now be necessary for Markham to find another messenger, once he ceases mourning the loss of his niece. The second, and far more important, one is that we have demonstrated to those ill-disposed towards our new King that we are a powerful force to be reckoned with. All in all, a successful operation, from which you may take some satisfaction in having played a minor role.'

'All I did was identify the messenger!' Oliver protested. 'I did not sign up with you in order to become some sort of stealthy assassin.' Cecil smiled back unpleasantly.

'Would you prefer that next time I equip you with a suitable weapon to enable you to dispatch your opponent face to face?'

'I am no murderer!' Oliver thundered as he leaped to his feet, but Cecil still appeared unmoved. 'You were once a soldier, were you not? You were paid to butcher to death the man in front of you, without regard to his political or religious views? If he was dressed in the livery of the enemy, did you hesitate, before running your blade through his guts, in order to first ascertain his identity, his age, his beliefs, and whether or not he possessed a wife and family? You are the worst form of hypocrite, Master Wade – you killed, in cold blood, those whom you had met for a brief second before ending their life with a swift thrust of a sword, or the sideways swish of an axe. And now you come whining to me because I brought about a more humane death – one that was at least inflicted on someone who I knew deserved it. Were you ever so scrupulous in identifying your victims?'

'You did not take the life of just one woman!' Oliver yelled in protest. 'Everyone else who was in that inn – other travellers, the innkeeper and his staff – not to mention seven innocent players in the theatre next door, whose only fault was to locate themselves in an adjacent building that for a brief moment contained someone whose life you commanded to be snuffed out.'

'Have you done with your hypocritical ravings, and may we now discuss your next mission?' Cecil enquired, seemingly unmoved by any of this. Oliver spat on the floor.

'*What* next mission? I have discharged my obligation to

you, have I not?' Cecil laughed.

'I was not aware that we placed any restriction of either time or nature on those tasks which I wish to set you. You have satisfactorily discharged the first of these, although you seem to take little comfort from that fact, and of course you are now even more beholden to me, unless you wish me to reveal to the authorities who was the last person to visit the inn before it disappeared in a hailstorm of wood and roof tiles.'

Oliver was shocked into silence, although sorely tempted to reach out and squeeze the last breath from the scrawny throat of the repulsive little reptile with so much power at his command. Cecil took his silence to be capitulation, and nodded towards the chair that Oliver had vacated in his anger.

'Unless your brains really *are* in your arse, as your futile protestations would seem to suggest, then you may find it easier to absorb what I have to instruct you in if you resume your seat.'

'This is the last time!' Oliver insisted, to a stern glare from Cecil as he advised him 'No it is not – it is merely the *next* time, so cease being so tedious and pay attention. Are you familiar with Buckinghamshire?'

'No,' Oliver insisted, partly in truth and partly out of a reluctance to become involved in more skulduggery. Cecil sighed heavily. 'Then your task will be made the more difficult, since a week from today I wish you to travel to a place called Luffield. It is in the north of the county, and closer to Northampton than it is to London. Allow at least one day for travel, then stay overnight in some convenient hostelry.'

'Convenient for you to blow up?' Oliver enquired sourly, but Cecil smiled. 'Should the need arise to have you eliminated, believe me when I say that I will choose some method far more direct, and easy to organise. Do you know how difficult it is to acquire gunpowder since the Armada was defeated?'

'Assuming that I deign to travel to this "Luffield" place,' Oliver replied, ignoring what was probably only intended as a rhetorical question anyway, 'then what do you wish of me?'

'You will journey to the ruins of the disused priory there, and meet with a man called John Gerard. You have heard of him?'

'No,' Oliver replied with heavy sarcasm, 'but I would wager that he has never heard of me either.'

'He has, however, heard of Nicholas Bray, who is the man you will pretend to be,' Cecil advised him. 'You are from an impoverished line of gentry, reduced to working as an intermediary for a powerful and wealthy Courtier with Catholic sympathies who can finance a covert journey to Spain for Gerard and a few of his followers, who wish to impress upon King Philip the need to keep increased tolerance for Catholics high on the list of demands in return for a peace treaty with our own King James.'

'And this John Gerard is a Catholic, I assume?' Oliver enquired listlessly, already bored with the proposed mission. Cecil laughed out loud. 'The worst sort. He is a Jesuit, and the leader of a powerful band of practising Catholics.'

'And presumably you wish me to ferret out some valuable information from him regarding his followers?' Oliver enquired in the same bored tone, then snapped back to attention when he received Cecil's answer. 'No – I wish you to obtain from him further information about the same group of Catholics whose comely messenger disappeared in a fountain of debris in Southwark two nights ago.' Then Cecil allowed himself a superior smirk as he saw Oliver trying to reconcile all this conflicting information in his head.

'Why would a devout Catholic be prepared to divulge information regarding a group of fellow Catholics that will undoubtedly lead them into your clutches?' was the question that Oliver eventually framed, and Cecil nodded. 'A very perceptive question.'

'And do you intend to supply me with a very perceptive answer?' Oliver demanded, and again Cecil nodded.

'There are two groups of Catholics currently here in England, and fortunately for us they are locked in disagreement for reasons into which we need not descend. The first you have already encountered indirectly, in that it is led by the William Watson who is currently inside The Clink, and who was, until your timely interference with his arrangements, in regular communication with Sir Griffin Markham, whose niece was employed as the messenger between them. We believe that Markham and his associates are plotting something against our new King, with a view to obtaining greater concessions towards their faith. We are not aware of precisely what form that plot will take, but I clearly wish it suppressed before it comes to the ears of the King himself, who will either order harsh reprisals that might throw the nation into further religious turmoil, or hold me responsible for the fact that it was allowed to develop in the first place.'

'And the other group?' Oliver enquired, although he believed that he already had the answer to that question.

'The other group is led by Gerard, and prefers to bring pressure to bear on King James through the hand of the Spanish King Philip. They are apprehensive that any ill-advised plot by Markham's group will lead to the reprisals of which I just spoke, and they wish to take the credit when greater tolerance for Catholics becomes part of the proposed peace treaty between England and Spain.'

'So those two groups have no love for each other?'

'Not even any regard, to the extent that Gerard has come forward to alert us to the fact that Markham's group are plotting something.'

Oliver's scepticism was evident in his next question. 'Why would an ardent Catholic such as Gerard choose to do business with the very government that is holding down freedom of worship the Roman way?' Cecil's returning smile almost qualified as a leer.

'He does not. Gerard believes that he is dealing with Henry Howard, Earl of Northampton, the second son of the Duke of Norfolk who was executed by the former King Henry, and the younger brother of the current Duke of Norfolk. The Howard family have long been suspected of Catholic sympathies, despite their protestations to the contrary, and Gerard was easily duped into believing that the information he has to impart will be welcomed by a man of influence in the new King's Council. If our plans come to fruition, and this Markham plot is suppressed, I shall of course advise his Majesty that I was the one responsible for same, but should ought go awry, then the name of Howard would not be difficult to drop in the appropriate ear.'

Oliver's head was ringing with all this information, and his blood was chilling from the realisation of just how amoral and devious his unwanted employer was capable of being.

'This "Nicholas Bray" that you wish me to impersonate is presumably intended to be a messenger from this Henry Howard?' Oliver enquired by way of confirmation, and when Cecil smiled and nodded he added 'May I presume that he does not in fact exist?'

'Not until you bring him to life with your actor's skilful guile,' Cecil advised him. 'You will pretend to be high born, but living in reduced circumstances, the third son of an impoverished estate somewhere in Devon, or perhaps Shropshire - wherever your mind takes a fancy to. You meet with Gerard, take from him what he has to impart regarding the Markham intrigue, and report it back to me. I do not propose to impose a time limit on your return, but your meeting with Gerard has been arranged for noon a week today – a Saturday - so if you are not back here by the following, say, Tuesday, you know what to expect. You will find that my senior clerk Coleman out there has a bag with money for your necessary outlays, but do not fritter it all on the comeliest looking whore. A horse will be placed at your disposal from my stables, and I imagine that your theatre wardrobe contains the necessary attire for the country gentleman of limited means that you will pretend to be. God speed - or God help - you.'

***

Oliver tied his horse to the rusting gate post, allowing it a long lead rope so that it might forage through the waist high grass that he crept cautiously through, his hand hovering nervously over his sword hilt, just in case. He now trusted Cecil as much as he believed in fairies, and this could be an elegant plot to silence a man who knew the real cause of the

Southwark explosion.

Ahead of him lay the ivy-covered ruins of what must once have been a magnificent house of God, to judge by the height of the remaining three walls of its main chapel. The ornately carved stones that he occasionally encountered almost hidden in the long grass as he made his cautious way towards it suggested that it had not yet fallen prey to locals intent on rebuilding their more humble dwellings; on the other hand, he reasoned, this was a remote rural setting, and he had encountered few signs of habitation on his short journey from the inn in which he had spent a restless night, wondering if it too was marked for an explosion.

He came to what must once have been the western entrance to the former chapel, peered cautiously inside, then drew back quickly as he spotted a man kneeling before what was left of its altar. The man appeared to be deep in prayer, but one could not be too cautious in the line of work in which Oliver was unwillingly engaged, and others might be lurking within the recesses that lined the former nave. Then his blood chilled as the man spoke.

'I have finished my devotions, whoever you may be. God be with you, and do not fear to approach.' Then he rose from his kneeling position, turned and looked back down the nave at Oliver. 'My name is John,' he added. 'And what might your name be?'

'I am Nicholas,' Oliver lied, 'and I am here to meet a man named John. Might you be he?'

The man smiled and walked halfway back down the nave towards him. 'Come further inside, if we wish not to be seen together.'

Oliver did as requested, but still looked nervously from

side to side as he passed decaying pillars behind which assassins might be waiting. The man smiled more broadly as he seemed to read Oliver's mind. 'We are alone,' he reassured him. 'Were it not so, I would have been dead long ere you found me. Who sent you?'

'An English earl,' Oliver replied guardedly, hoping that this time at least he would remember his lines. The man nodded. 'Of which county is he the Earl?'

'Northampton,' Oliver replied with a smile of his own. 'I am Nicholas Bray, and I believe that you have something of value to impart to my master.'

'I have indeed,' the man replied, 'but before I do so, have you been advised of my true identity?'

'I was told that your name is John Gerard, and that you are a member of the Society of Jesus.'

'And you come alone? I am well aware that there was one horse tied at the gate back there, but how do I know that there are not others?'

'You do not,' Oliver smiled back, 'any more than I may be certain that you do not have men of your own concealed in this ruin.'

'There are none, on my word as a man of God,' Gerard sighed, 'but your choice of word aptly describes the blasphemous desecration of what was once a thriving Benedictine house. Given that your master misguidedly pretends to follow the Protestant path, I may assume that you are similarly misled, but you must both be advised that the gates of Hell are open wide to receive the persecutors of the true faith.'

'That is presumably not why we are met,' Oliver replied drily. 'I have been forewarned of my doom by many a man such as yourself, but for the present I would learn what it is that you have to advise my master, then I would take my leave of you.'

'Very well,' Gerard agreed. 'Inform him that there is a plot to kidnap the new King.'

The look on Oliver's face betrayed his shock, and Gerard smiled yet again. 'You wish to know how I came by this intelligence?'

'Of course,' Oliver confirmed. 'It is, after all, a most disturbing revelation.'

'Quite simply, I was invited to become a part of it, by a man in York who feels slighted by King James's failure to promote him to a higher clerical office in the Protestant community in which he currently holds only a minor prebend. I of course declined.'

'The name of this man?'

'Sir George Brooke.'

'And he is a Protestant, you say? Why would he approach a Catholic such as yourself – and a Jesuit, what is more - in order to foment rebellion, when as a Protestant he must be your sworn enemy?' Gerard gave a wry smile before replying.

'Would that matters were so simple. Brooke is a man who changes his religious loyalties whenever he deems it appropriate. For some years it has suited his ambition to wear Protestant colours, but he was raised as a Catholic, and has many friends who have never traded their faith for advancement. As a result, Brooke has the ear of many wealthy Catholics who are seeking to shake the trees of power for the fruit that may fall from them. One of those fruits is of course greater recognition of their right to worship as Catholics behind a facade of Protestant conformity, and a man such as Brooke is a perfect front for them. Brooke may have been led to believe that he is supported by Catholics who share his belief that he has been under-rewarded for his service to the realm, but they are in fact seeking to hide behind his respectability in order to get close to the new King.'

'And when they do?' Oliver enquired with foreboding, but Gerard shrugged. 'It depends who you ask, but I have learned, by means that need not concern you, that one of Brooke's leading supporters – a man called Markham, with an estate further to the north of here – has hatched a plot to kidnap his Majesty and hold him to ransom until he accedes to their demands for greater religious freedom.'

'Sir Griffin Markham, of Nottinghamshire?' Oliver enquired with a sharp intake of breath and Gerard nodded. 'You clearly already know of the man.'

'By reputation only,' Oliver insisted as several facts fell into place at the same time. 'They say that he is in communication with the man Watson, who is currently inside The Clink.'

'The very same. Watson is another who sets himself up as a leader of Catholics, but he is leading them all into certain discovery and death. He is very strong in rhetoric, but singularly lacking in either deep thought or rational reason. The planned kidnap of the King can result in only death to the would-be kidnappers.'

'And you clearly have no high regard for either the man or his followers,' Oliver reminded him, 'so what is it that you seek from my master? Why not simply let them blunder on and get themselves hung, drawn and quartered, or perhaps burned at the stake?'

'For one thing they are fellow observers of the true faith, and I cannot sit idly by and watch them slaughtered for no good reason,' Gerard replied. 'God knows we already have enough martyrs not to require any more. But secondly, and perhaps even closer to my own hopes and aspirations, any attempt on the King's person can result only in greater persecution of those who share my hopes for the reconciliation of the English Church with that of Rome, and the return of the Pope's blessings on our humble worship.'

'So what do you require of my master, other than being placed in knowledge of what is being planned by this group led by Watson, Markham and Brooke?' Oliver enquired, and was somewhat taken aback when Gerard grasped his hand like a beggar seeking alms.

'He must do whatever lies within his power to prevent their plans going forward,' Gerard urged him. 'If it be possible, the plot must be thwarted without the good name of God's true faith being associated with it. Your master has the King's ear, and may well be able to divert suspicion away from Catholics. Indeed, it may even lie within his power to seize those behind it before it goes much further and becomes generally known.'

'I shall see to it that he is swiftly made aware of this valuable information,' Oliver assured him. 'And in order to do so I must now take my departure and hasten back to London.'

'Do so with God's blessing,' Gerard mumbled gratefully, before raising his hand and pronouncing a few Latin words over Oliver's head.

The two men made their way separately out of the grounds

of the former priory, and Oliver occupied his return journey south wondering how his band of players were managing without him.

***

'You have done well,' Cecil conceded grudgingly as he sat absorbing the information that Oliver had brought back with him. 'And now you must journey much further north to ascertain how far these plans of Sir George Brooke have developed.'

'You obviously knew of him,' Oliver responded with distaste, 'since I did not give you the man's first name. If you knew what he was about, why did you waste my time in having it confirmed?'

'Because I *needed* it confirmed,' Cecil replied with irritation. 'The name of Brooke comes up regularly in intelligence that is brought to me, but until your meeting with Gerard I had no inkling of the precise nature of what they were planning. Now I must know when it is to be attempted, and who are its main players other than Markham and Brooke.'

'And you wish me to journey to Markham's estate?' Oliver enquired with resignation.

'No – to Brooke's residence in York,' Cecil insisted. 'You will be amply supplied for your travels, and you must adopt whatever disguise and false identity seems appropriate, but if I am to nip this blossoming plot in the bud, I must know how advanced it has become, and who are to be its executors.'

'I have my theatre to think of,' Oliver protested feebly, with no expectation of any favourable reaction. Even so, he was shocked and further sickened by the reaction he did receive.

'You also have your life to think of, Master Wade. You are

now, in the eyes of any interrogator employed by his Majesty, not only a deserter from his army, and the last person seen to visit a certain inn in Southwark before it exploded with the loss of thirteen lives, but you have been seen meeting with John Gerard, a dangerous Jesuit who has been evading capture for some years now. His life is forfeit if he is caught, and you may rely on my assurance that it would be a source of no regret to me to add you to the list of those to be burned at Smithfield as a known associate of his.'

'You are less than a bastard,' Oliver snarled as he rose to leave. 'At least bastards have mothers who love them.'

Chapter Four

The players sat disconsolately around the large table in the main room of The Cardinal as they absorbed Oliver's latest news. Matthew Partridge was not complaining, since as understudy to every actor in the company he was getting a lot of time on stage playing the parts that Oliver had written for himself. But for the remainder it was a worrying time, since Oliver in person always attracted a sizeable crowd, and every penny counted when the admission money had to be shared between a dozen of them.

'Who knows?' Oliver added in an attempt to lift the communal spirit. 'I may not be gone all that long, and the new play has a major character who's a woman anyway.'

'I only hope I can carry it off,' Meg Tyler muttered, 'since we've only got three days to rehearse it, and even though I've been plaguing you for months to write me the part of "The Maid of Orleans", I wasn't really ready to go on stage with such little notice.'

'At least you won't have to wave your duckies around,' Tim Bryant observed drily, but Meg was not in the mood to be consoled. 'It's my best look,' she argued, 'and I'm not sure that I can play the saint all that convincingly. But at least we won't be visited by the authorities – or will we?' she enquired of Oliver, who shook his head reassuringly. 'Probably not, since I'm off doing things for those best placed to close us down.'

'Why exactly *are* you heading north?' Giles Banting enquired, and Oliver shook his head more vigorously. 'I'm not allowed to say, but it's important to people who matter. You'll just have to trust me, and while I'm away I can work on that new comedy we talked about. But do any of you know what a "prebend" is, exactly?'

'I do,' Martin Amesbury admitted, almost shamefacedly. 'It's money paid to a clergyman who earns his living serving a diocese. He's called a "prebendary", but why do you need to know?'

'And how do *you* know?' Meg enquired teasingly, and Martin hung his head in embarrassment. 'I was once hoping to become a priest. Then I met a girl with duckies like yours.' The rest of the company hooted with laughter, and Meg wished she'd kept her mouth shut. But Oliver chose to answer the original question, since he needed all the help he could get with his latest unwelcome mission for Cecil.

'I need to know how I can get closer to a man who's a "prebendary", in a place up north. Preferably by becoming one of his household or something, since I need to be able to learn the identities of those who come and go from the man's house.'

'He probably lives somewhere within the grounds of the church that he's attached to,' Martin advised him, 'so that won't be easy. As a clergyman with a modest living he probably has a small household. He may be married, of course, since that's allowed in the Church these days, and if so his wife will organise the servants. If not, then probably his Steward, if he's wealthy enough to employ one.' Oliver frowned.

'Would such a man entertain visiting scholars?' he enquired as a thought came to him, and Martin nodded. 'Almost certainly, but you'll need to be convincing if he engages you in theological debate. Better, perhaps, to be a poet or a writer on Biblical themes. You're halfway there anyway, as a playwright.' Oliver grinned.

'I don't think he'd be too impressed if he learned that half my plays have Meg dangling her duckies for public exhibition. It's a good suggestion, however – perhaps I'll pretend that I'm searching for inspiration for a new mystery play or something.'

'If by any chance you're travelling to York,' Martin advised him 'then you'll probably be well received by anyone with High Church leanings, but make sure to keep your writings conforming. They had a series of mystery plays up there that were banned by Queen Elizabeth in her early years, and it became heresy to perform them.'

'All the more reason why they might welcome a new collection,' Oliver smiled, 'and my grateful thanks for that most valuable assistance. Perhaps you should take the part of the Pope in the new play.'

'A Pope misled from his true calling by the sight of a pair of duckies?' Meg quipped, and during the ensuing laughter Oliver took the opportunity to slip sadly away.

***

A week later, with a sinking heart and a vague feeling that he was getting into more intrigue than was good for him, Oliver hitched his weary horse to the rail and walked up to the liveried servant who stood with a bored expression at the opening that led into what looked like a town all of its own inside the environs of York. In its centre was the magnificent Minster of St Peter, and the approach to it was through a massive cobbled courtyard that was itself dotted with buildings, while along the interior of the walls to the side and front could be seen rows of houses.

Oliver took the obvious step, hoping that he would not seem too out of place in this holy enclave. He walked up to the elderly retainer at the entrance and enquired where he might find Sir George Brooke. The man looked puzzled for a moment, then his eyes lit up in recognition. 'You must mean Canon Brooke!' he replied in a thick North Country accent that Oliver had become more familiar with during his long journey north.

'That must be him,' Oliver nodded, 'so where will I find him?' The man nodded towards the massive church. 'Probably in there, preparing for the evening Mass. Not the proper one, of course, but there you go – must keep within the law, mustn't we?'

Nodding a vague agreement, Oliver obtained leave to walk his horse over the cobbles until he reached a stables of sorts to the side of the main church and left his horse with the boy who appeared to be in charge, when he was not toying with a knife and a piece of wood. Inside the huge cathedral Oliver was immediately aware of a substantial drop in temperature, and put his shivering down to that, rather than any sense of foreboding that he was not about to admit to, even to himself. The action was spotted by a priest of some sort, dressed in a plain black soutane, who walked over and smiled kindly down at Oliver as he took a seat in a pew near the back of the building while he adjusted his eyes to the gloom after the bright sunset that he'd left outside.

'Are you a poor traveller in need of alms, or the hospitality of our humble house?' the man enquired in a kindly voice, and Oliver was touched by the man's humanity.

'A traveller certainly,' Oliver replied in what he hoped was a scholarly tone, 'and only as poor as a wandering playwright can be in these straightened times.' The man's smile faded as he looked down at Oliver disparagingly. 'It is as well that those who promote bawdiness in our new theatres do not thrive, but perhaps a while longer spent in supplication in this house of God will enable you to hear His voice calling you from your wicked ways. Until then, I leave you in the tranquillity of His grace.'

'I'm not that sort of playwright,' Oliver advised the man urgently before he could move away. 'In truth, my reason for travelling to York was in the hope that my services might be required for the restoration of your mystery plays. I was never in holy orders like yourself, but I have already heard the word of God, and he called me into His service employing my humble talents as a writer on spiritual themes.'

'I am only a lay brother,' the man smiled, 'but you should speak to Canon Brooke, since it would seem that you and he share an interest. He's the man in front of the altar, replacing the candles, and he has aspirations to restore the tradition of performing mystery plays. I'll ask him to come and speak to you when he's completed his work, but before the start of Evensong.'

A few minutes later Oliver was approached, where he sat with his head bowed in pretended prayer, by a tall, thin faced man well advanced in his years who wore a gold cincture over a plain white alb, tucked under which was a purple stole.

'You are he who shares my hope that the mystery plays will once again be offered here to the glory of God?' he enquired, and Oliver adopted a weary smile as he nodded. 'You are, I hope, Canon Brooke? If not, then my journey has been in vain.'

'I am he,' Brooke replied with a smile. 'By whom were you sent?'

'A lady of my acquaintance who shared my love of masques dedicated to God's work,' Oliver lied convincingly. 'Mistress Harriet Markham?'

A look of concern crossed Brooke's face. 'You speak as if she has departed this world – or did you mean to imply that you and she are no longer close?'

Oliver's sad look in reply was not entirely the product of his actor's guile. 'You will not have heard, perhaps, but she died tragically some weeks ago. She was on one of her regular sojourns in London when the inn at which she was residing was blown up in some dastardly revenge by Protestant butchers.'

Brooke involuntarily crossed himself and muttered a few words in Latin that betrayed his true allegiance. 'You and she were close?' he enquired politely, and Oliver nodded. 'Not as close as I might have wished, given her great beauty, but close enough for her uncle – who mourns her still – to suggest that I might journey north and assuage my grief at her death by embarking upon the works of devotion that we had long discussed. I speak – if I might make so bold, and trust in your discretion – of the restoration of the mystery play tradition for which this beautiful house of God was once famous throughout Christendom.'

Brooke beamed appreciatively and muttered some more Latin before indicating the altar with a jerk of his head. 'I must shortly assist in the divine evening service, but if you would care to partake in it, along with the congregation that will shortly begin to gather, I should be glad to offer you the hospitality of my humble board at the breaking of the evening bread. My house is but a few yards away, across the close that you must have traversed in order to enter the Minster.'

Oliver was warning himself that this was proving altogether too easy as he unpacked his few items of modest clothing in the chamber he had been allocated on the first floor of Canon Brooke's residence. It followed a modest supper, and a somewhat one-sided conversation in which Brooke disclosed a great deal of information about his 'life-long friend and one-time companion' Sir Griffin Markham, while Oliver avoided difficult questions on the same topic by claiming only to have really known his niece Harriet, and even then only in London. The false story he had invented for himself during the six day ride from London was employed to good effect as he convinced Brooke that he was about to begin what he regarded as his life's work – the retelling of the lives of the Christian martyrs by means of plays in the 'mystery' tradition that had made 'The York Cycle" so famous until banned by the ill-advised Elizabeth.

Whether it was this pious ambition, or the fact that Oliver – who was once again posing as 'Thomas Grange' – was apparently a friend of the Markham family of whom Brooke talked in tones of awed respect, the outcome had been precisely as Oliver had intended. He was now installed within Brooke's house, and all that was required of him was that he maintain the pretence of writing the first in his series of pageants regarding the lives of Christian saints. Given that he had already left 'The Martyrdom of the Maid of Orleans' with his company to bring alive back in the undercroft of The Cardinal this would prove no hardship, and he grinned to himself as he visualised the audience back in Shoreditch waiting expectantly for Meg Tyler's duckies to pop out of her bodice on the funeral pyre.

Three weeks elapsed before Oliver became seriously bored in his assumed role. From time to time he had descended down to the supper table to share with the eager George Brooke the latest instalment of the saga of Joan of Arc that he had re-written from memory, taking great pains to make it more worshipful than the original, in which he had played to the masses with scenes suggestive of French foot soldiers lusting after the simple country girl dressed in battle leggings and a breastplate that was more suggestive than protective. Brooke seemed content – even enthusiastic – with what his free boarder was producing, and only his elderly housekeeper Maude seemed to resent the presence of the handsome young house guest, possibly because his very appearance brought home to her on a daily basis what she had forfeited by choosing to open her heart to God rather than her legs to a husband.

But during those three weeks there had been regular visits from a retainer from the Markham estate called Robert Drysdale, who had joined them for meals during his stay. This had drawn heavily on Oliver's powers of deceit and impersonation as he posed as a friend of the late Harriet Markham, avoiding awkward questions from Drysdale regarding his familiarity with the rest of the Markham family. Oliver thanked his lucky stars that the original story he had fed to Brooke required him only to have known Harriet during her London visits, and he remembered enough about her physical appearance and the little she had told him about her life for him to maintain the pretence of having been a close friend of hers. From Drysdale Oliver learned that Sir

Griffin Markham was still in deep mourning for the loss of his niece, and he had seemed to allay suspicions further by implying that he was aware that Harriet had been visiting London only in order to carry messages backwards and forwards to William Watson in The Clink, but had done nothing to betray her.

On the fourth visit by Drysdale, there was a distinct change in the atmosphere in the house – a vague, ill-defined but palpable tension that had not marked any of Drysdale's previous arrivals and departures. Oliver had not seen Drysdale arrive, and when invited to join the two men for supper he looked around as hard as he dared for any sign of the familiar satchel that he assumed always carried messages between the two conspirators. It was nowhere to be seen, and when he spotted Maude eyeing him curiously as his eyes wandered everywhere around the small all-purpose sitting room he gave up looking and listened more attentively to the conversation between Drysdale and Brooke. They clearly did not yet trust him as much as he would have hoped, since the exchanges between them were carefully guarded, even cryptic.

'How does your master as he prepares himself for travel?' Brooke enquired, and Drysdale was clearly choosing his words with caution as he responded with 'He hopes to rid himself finally of his grieving with the satisfaction of a journey whose outcome will be a fitting tribute to the tireless efforts of his niece in the matter that is so close to both your hearts. He is also happily anticipating your reunion.'

'Tell him that my heart is gladdened by that prospect, and that we shall meet where previously agreed,' Brooke replied with an anxious smile. With that the conversation moved on to discussions regarding how the Archbishop might best be approached for his consent to the staging of 'Master Grange's' new mystery play.

They were clearly approaching the conclusion of whatever the two conspirators had been planning for some time, and Oliver's heart beat a little stronger as he lay on his bolster in the upper room, wondering how best to convey this warning to Cecil. He found that sleep eluded him for most of the night, and he was still dozing fitfully when he came fully awake to the sound of Maude serving breakfast downstairs. The sun had barely risen, and Brooke himself was an inveterate sleeper-in, so Oliver could only surmise that the man up and about was Drysdale. He hastily threw his outer clothing on and wandered downstairs, barely having to fake the yawn that was part of his impersonation of a man who had risen early. Maude was her usual surly self as she cleared a space for Oliver at the table and disappeared into the kitchen to acquire more herring to go with the manchet loaf that Drysdale had already broken into.

A few carefully loaded questions obtained the information that Oliver was seeking – the man was heading back south after only one night in York, and there was every possibility that he was conveying important information from Brooke. Oliver urgently needed to know what that was, but the absence of any satchel suggested that this latest exchange of intelligence had been by word of mouth only. Even so, there might be something – a document, a map, something – in Brooke's small study that might give a clue to what was about to occur, and as soon as Drysdale had risen from the table and headed to his room to collect his riding cloak and boots, Oliver also slipped from his seat and glided swiftly into the study.

He heard the sound of Maude offering an apology to Drysdale that she had been unable to wake 'the master' from a deep slumber, then wishing their guest 'God Speed', and in the belief that she would be fully engaged in clearing the breakfast table Oliver began shuffling urgently through the papers on Brooke's study desk. Some of them were religious texts, and a few appeared to be letters from Markham that referred guardedly to 'our great venture', without anything further to indicate what that might be.

At that moment Oliver heard a sharp intake of breath from the doorway, and turned guiltily to the sight of Maude with her eyes wide open, before they narrowed in accusation.

'I always thought there was somethin' about you that weren't quite right,' she hissed accusingly, 'and now I finds you tryin' to steal from the Master what's always treated you kindly, like the good Christian soul that he is! When he gets up I'll be tellin' him what you been up to, and then you'll be out of here on your thievin' backside.'

'I'll save you the trouble,' Oliver replied, grim-faced as he pushed heavily past her and ran for the door. Fortunately he'd dressed for travel when he first heard Drysdale up and about downstairs, and guessed that he was heading south that morning. His first thought had been to follow him back to the Markham estate, and it was only when he could find no recent message in Brooke's papers that he realised that he now had a more urgent reason to pursue the man. He raced to the stables and handed the dim-witted boy five marks in exchange for the information he needed, which the lad was only too willing to supply.

'He went out by the south road, Master. He must be headin'

for Selby or somewhere.'

Thanking him curtly, Oliver leaped into the saddle as the boy handed him the reins, then thundered across the cobbles and out into Peter Gate, scattering passers-by who leapt to one side to avoid the pounding hooves. Down through the main town and over the stone bridge that spanned the Ouse, he was clear of the ancient town within minutes, then pulled hard on the reins as he saw a figure on horseback less than half a league ahead of him. The man was wearing a feathered green bonnet like that worn by Drysdale when he'd arrived the previous evening, and Oliver would need to trust to his belief that he was following the right man until he could confront him somewhere more remote than a public road in open country.

That opportunity came in the late afternoon, when the man he was pursuing finally came to a halt after a tedious all-day journey, and handed his horse's bridle to the ostler of an inn in Selby called 'The Malt Shovel'. Oliver would now need to wait until night fell.

He was fortunate that the inn had only two rooms available for travellers, and shortly before the establishment closed for the night Oliver presented himself at the kitchen door and asked to speak to the landlord. An overweight man with a black beard and a dirty apron stepped out into the courtyard, and Oliver drew his sword menacingly as he announced that he was in the King's service, and was in pursuit of a spy posing as a nobleman's messenger, and calling himself 'Drysdale'.

'Don't want no trouble from 'is Majesty,' the landlord replied, wide-eyed with fear at the sight of Oliver's sword point only inches from his throat. 'You'll find the man in the back room upstairs, and mind an' mention my loyalty should it be questioned. I 'ad no idea who he were, I swear!'

'You may rest at ease,' Oliver assured him as he entered the kitchen, sword still drawn, then raced through the parlour and up the stairs. The door to the upstairs rear room was partly ajar, and Oliver kicked it open with such force that it flew back off the side wall and came back towards him, necessitating that he kick it back open again more gently. Drysdale leapt from his pallet with a squawk of fear, then seemed to recognise Oliver.

'What means this rude intrusion?' he demanded, then froze as he saw the sword. Oliver wasted no time.

'I am, as you will now surmise, no mere writer of religious plays. I am employed by the King's Secretary, Master Cecil, and I will run you through without a second thought unless you tell me the nature of your latest message to George Brooke.'

'What message?' Drysdale stalled, then screamed as Oliver slashed his sword point through the man's nightshirt. 'Mercy, I pray you!' Drysdale begged. 'It was but a short message, and it meant nought to me.'

'It will no doubt mean more to my noble master,' Oliver persisted, 'so what was it?'

'The business on which Brooke is embarked with my master is due to be conducted on 24th June next.'

'Unless you wish this point through your poxy throat,' Oliver bellowed, 'tell me the nature of that "business" without delay!'

'The kidnap of the King,' Drysdale croaked. 'As he journeys to Windsor.'

DAVID FIELD

Chapter Five

Plans for the coronation on 25th July were progressing nicely, but there was a worrying rift developing between James and his Council of State that Cecil was having the greatest difficulty in smoothing over. It all had to do with the title that James would assume.

The traditional title included a reference to Ireland, but there had hitherto been no need to mention Scotland, which had been separately governed. Now that the King of Scotland was also the King of England, a change was required in the formal address that would be boomed out from the altar of Westminster Abbey by Archbishop Whitgift when he presented their new monarch to his people at the culmination of the coronation ceremony. James had determined that he would be known as 'King of Great Britain', but this was being fervently opposed by Parliament, despite James's logical argument that the lands that he now ruled were 'compassed with one sea and of itself by nature indivisible.' The corresponding need to draft common laws for the one united nation was what the Members most distrusted, due in no large part to the ignorant tales that had drifted south from the common border regarding the lifestyles and personal habits of the supposed 'barbarians' to the north of it.

With his inbuilt disdain for anything that smacked of government by commoners, James had naturally looked to his small Council, led by Cecil, to support his boast of sitting on a combined throne, and put Parliament in its place. But these were no longer the days when Parliament could be either ignored or manipulated, and the members of Council were not entirely united in their support for an incomer who was only indirectly of Tudor blood, and rumoured to be about to alienate the still powerful Catholic minor nobility.

Following the latest bad tempered exchange between King and Council, that James had brought to an abrupt end by storming out, red faced, with Cecil scuttling close on his heels, the atmosphere in the Audience Chamber was chilly and hostile.

'Can these ignorant fools not see the justice of my arguments, man?' James demanded of Cecil, who shook his head sadly and murmured 'They can see it, Your Majesty – it is simply the case that they cannot share it.'

'And who are they to be gainsaying whatever title their King appointed by God should choose to take upon himself?' James demanded, like a child bewailing the injustice of being denied a favourite toy. 'Did God not appoint me to sit above them in all things? Do they defy God's will? If so, can they not see that they court eternal damnation?'

'If we might discuss the progress to Windsor, Your Majesty?' Cecil offered in a vain attempt to divert the flow of wrath before it ended once again in a denunciation of any form of democratic government, but James waved his hand angrily in the air in a sign of dismissal.

'If that is your best response, Cecil, then you may withdraw from the presence. You are no better than the rest – how do I know that you also are not plotting against me?'

'There are no plots among the more senior nobles, Your Majesty,' Cecil insisted, but the royal glare did not lessen. 'And the *minor* ones, Cecil? What know you of plots among the minor nobility, who are greater in number, and what steps have you taken to suppress them?'

'I have my spies working throughout the realm, Your Majesty,' Cecil assured him, 'and you shall be advised when plots are revealed, and those who lie behind them are brought to justice.'

'But you have so far brought me none, have you?' James replied accusingly. 'For aught I know, they lie behind this unfathomable refusal of my Council to assent to the simple matter of the title that I would assume. If they begrudge me that, how can I not suspect that they too plot against my very presence on the throne?'

'You may be assured that they do not, Your Majesty,' Cecil wheedled unconvincingly, but James was beyond reassurance.

'It was better when I ruled only Scotland, and had about me men that I could trust because of the love that we bore each other,' he countered hotly. 'Perhaps the time is meet for me to bring them south to rule England also, instead of this surly crew of high-born ingrates who cling to their ancient titles while denying me the simplest of my desires.'

Cecil's heart almost stopped as he took in the implications of what James was threatening. Rumours had been rife, long before Cecil had connived behind the back of the dying Elizabeth to bring James south as her successor, of the Scots King's preference for favourites who hung around his throne in Stirling Castle. It was even reliably alleged that their favoured status owed much to their good looks, and that James had indulged in affairs 'contrary to nature' with some of them. By the date of his entry into London, its riverside taverns had a new set of bawdy jests regarding his sexuality, epitomised by the one that asserted that 'Elizabeth was King, now James is Queen'. It was equally offensive towards the late Queen, of course, but Cecil could not for one moment contemplate the possibility that the ears closest to the King's would be located on Palace bolsters.

'Your Majesty may rest assured that you are loyally served by those here in England who have your best interests at heart.'

'May I?' James demanded testily. 'May I *really*? Perhaps I will be more inclined to believe that when I see some of these alleged nobles in chains at my feet, begging for my clemency. And they had better be minor ones, Cecil, or you will hear more from me!'

It was barely an hour after this unsettling audience with the King that Cecil, still located on an upper floor of Whitehall Palace where he was inspecting the security arrangements, was advised that Oliver Wade was downstairs, and wishing to speak urgently with him.

'Escort him up here,' Cecil instructed two of the guards closest to him, and they accompanied the clerk back downstairs, reappearing a few minutes later with an eager and satisfied looking Oliver. Cecil steered him into a side chamber, and instructed the guards who had brought him up to wait outside for further orders. He indicated that Oliver should take one of the ornate chairs, and smiled as he noticed him admiring the plush surroundings.

'Part of the Palace that I warrant you have never seen before,' Cecil smiled with self-satisfaction. 'It is the sort of luxury you can afford when you have risen as high in the royal service as I have. Now, what news?'

'All good, my Lord,' Oliver assured him with a broad

smile. 'I travelled to the house of Sir George Brooke – or "Canon Brooke", as he seems to prefer to be addressed – and can confirm that he received regular visits from a messenger employed by Sir Griffin Markham. The man is called Robert Drysdale, and I intercepted him at an inn during his return journey to the Markham estate. I forced him at sword point to reveal that there is a plot to kidnap the King, and that it is timed for 24th June, when apparently his Majesty will be travelling to Windsor.'

'Excellent!' Cecil sighed. 'I can ensure that there is additional protection for his Majesty when he undertakes that brief journey, which is less than a day's ride. I will ensure that he is so closely guarded that not even a cannon shot could penetrate his entourage.'

'But surely those who are behind this plot will not now proceed with it, in the knowledge that they are discovered?' Oliver argued, and Cecil frowned. 'How can that be, if the messenger be dead? I assume that he delivered the message to Brooke, and that Brooke will proceed to meet up with Markham not knowing that their messenger is no more? Or do you believe that Markham will grow suspicious when this man Drysdale does not return?'

Oliver was puzzled, and without realising the error he was about to make, enquired 'Why would Drysdale not return and advise Markham that the plot is discovered?'

'He is dead, surely?' Cecil demanded with a darkening countenance as the truth began to dawn on him. Oliver shook his head. 'I didn't kill him. It would have been a pointless waste of human life, after he had told me what I wanted to know.'

'So presumably you brought him back here as your

prisoner?' Cecil demanded in mounting disbelief, but Oliver shook his head. 'I allowed him his freedom for the very reason I gave a moment ago. He will return to his master, warn him that the plot has been discovered, and it will not go ahead. His Majesty will remain safe, which is what we were seeking to achieve, was it not?'

Cecil's face darkened from its original hue of light red until it was almost purple, and for a moment he seemed lost for words as he struggled to draw breath. But he finally overcame his temporary disability and emitted a loud howl of rage.

'You stupid fucking cretin! You have allowed the plotters to learn that they have been discovered, and have brought no-one back that I may throw at his Majesty's feet as proof of our skilful work. Not even a corpse!'

'Of what value would have been a corpse?' Oliver enquired flippantly, finally sending Cecil over the edge. He called for the guards to re-enter the chamber and seize Oliver, then screamed at him as he stood with both arms pinioned.

'Idiot! Numbskull! Moron! Of all the dithering fucking shit-brains I could have employed, I chose the worst! You have failed dismally, and you may look forward to nothing but the Tower, and eventual execution for treason!'

'How can it be treason if I have saved an attempt on the King's person?' Oliver enquired in his lingering naivety, and Cecil foamed at the mouth in his response.

'It matters not that the King has been preserved if I cannot bring him proof of that! You bring me second-hand stories only – words that are no better than your standing in society, which as an actor of filthy plays is not very high. To convince the King I needed heads that I could place on spikes. Perhaps

I can retrieve something from your blundering by making it yours. Take him away and have him conveyed to the Tower!'

Chapter Six

Cecil had calmed down considerably by the time that he brought his horse to a halt at the entrance gate to the Lower Ward of Windsor Castle and announced his identity, demanding entry in the name of the King. He and his modest escort were granted immediate admission, and within minutes he was being welcomed into the Salisbury Tower by the man who had his residence there, the Captain of the Palace Guard, William Wade.

'It is gratifying to find you in such obvious rude health,' Cecil replied to Wade's warm welcome. 'My father always spoke highly of your service to England in those uncertain days of the Scots Mary and the intrigues in France. He advised me, before his death, that you were for some years in the covert employ of Sir Francis Walsingham, to whom you proved invaluable in the smoking out of Jesuits. Presumably you rejoice to see that England's throne is once again occupied by a confirmed Protestant, and to be so placed as to preserve his life and liberty in this most royal of residences.'

Wade looked him firmly in the eye as he grinned back at him. 'You have clearly inherited your father's talent for coming at a matter sideways, Sir Robert. I assume that your presence here today concerns a matter touching the King's safety?'

'Indeed it does, Captain,' Cecil smiled encouragingly, 'but in truth it is two matters.'

'I will let you select the order in which you raise them,' Wade continued to grin confidently, while gesturing for

Cecil to take the other available seat in front of the fire as he poured him a mug of mulled wine from the jug on the table between them.

'The first is routine enough, for a man such as yourself,' Cecil assured him. 'The King is due to journey here on 24th June for two weeks of hunting in the royal park before he faces the rigours attendant upon his coronation. I believe that an attempt may be made to kidnap him as he journeys here, and it is my instruction to you that you have a party of armed men under your command ride out to meet him at an early stage in his journey, and certainly no further west than Chelsea.'

'Will he not have his usual Yeoman Bodyguard escort from the Tower?' Wade enquired with a look of alarm, but Cecil nodded reassuringly. 'He will, of course, but I wish to ensure that the bodyguard that day is so heavy as he ventures further into open country that no attempt to kidnap him would be likely to succeed.'

'And yet you only *suspect* that such an attempt will be made?' Wade enquired. 'How good is your intelligence in this regard?' Cecil sighed.

'I am certain that such an attempt was being planned, but cannot be sure that it has since been abandoned.' Wade's eyes narrowed.

'Your father – with Walsingham's able assistance, no doubt – would have resolved any remaining doubt on a matter so grave.' Cecil snorted with annoyance.

'So might I have done, were it not that the fool to whom I allocated the task, who confirmed the existence of the plot, but failed to either execute or apprehend the messenger who gave up the knowledge at the point of his sword. The messenger in question was allowed his freedom, and we cannot now be sure that he did not report back to his masters that the plot had been discovered. If he did, then clearly it will not take place. But if he has not yet done so, then the attempt on the King may still proceed.'

'And how long ago was this messenger intercepted?'

'Five days, at which point he still had at least a further two days of travel before he could reveal the discovery of the plot to his masters.'

'Then surely he has done so by now?' Wade reasoned, but Cecil shook his head. 'We cannot be certain of this, hence your second set of instructions.'

'You wish me to find the man, and bring him back into your custody?'

'No, I wish you to find him and kill him.'

'I am not a hired assassin,' Wade objected as his face darkened. 'I serve his Majesty in a protective capacity, and should there be any attempt on his life or his liberty, then rest assured that I would willingly risk my own mortal existence. But I do not slaughter on command.'

'I rather think that you can be persuaded to do so on this occasion,' Cecil grinned ominously. 'You will seek out this man, whose name is Robert Drysdale, and who serves Sir Griffin Markham on his estate in North Nottinghamshire. A place called Ollerton. You will then torture him, if necessary, in order to ascertain whether or not he has alerted the plotters to the fact that they have been exposed, and regardless of his answer you will then kill him and bring his body back here, that I may place it on public display as the price of treason.'

Wade rose abruptly from his chair and stood over Cecil, who appeared unmoved as his host raised his voice in angry refusal. 'Your father would never have demanded such unworthy actions of me! I am no man's butcher, and what you ask is as much a smear on your own character as it would be on mine, were I to stoop to agreeing to it.'

'Perhaps you should first acquaint yourself with the identity of the idiot who let this man Drysdale escape in the first place, and who is even now languishing in the Tower under suspicion of treason.'

'I care not *who* he might be!' Wade replied angrily. 'I am bound to observe that whoever he is, his fault lies in failing to secure his man, and not in treason. Perhaps he shares my abhorrence of the needless taking of human life. Since when did that become treasonous?'

Cecil smiled horribly as he delivered the verbal blow. 'He may well share your obvious reluctance to act in the King's best interests, Captain Wade, since I am advised that such weakness often runs in families.'

'Your meaning?'

'My meaning is that the man who currently languishes in the Tower shares not only your scruple regarding the taking of life, but also your name. He was once a soldier, I am told, but in recent years he has sunk to the level of staging acts of public lewdness in what he chooses to describe as a theatre in Shoreditch.'

William Wade's jaw dropped. 'You refer to my son Oliver?'

'I do indeed, Captain,' Cecil replied triumphantly. 'Time to restore the family honour, I believe.'

***

Oliver cowered fearfully in a corner of his cell in the Beauchamp Tower as the door ground open and in the shadows a tall man was granted entry. Oliver kept his eyes on the floor, fearful of seeing whatever instrument of torture the man might have in his hand. He had been warned that it was only a matter of time before steps were taken to 'put him to the question', and he had not the remotest idea what that question might be, even less what answer he would be required to give. Then he looked up sharply as the man addressed him.

'Dear God, it's come to a merry pass! I thought that the day I buried your dear mother was the worst that I was ever to endure in this life, but the sight of you with your head bowed, languishing in the Tower accused of treason, must surely rank as a close second.'

'Father?' Oliver croaked as a wave of relief swept over him.

'I am he, although I am surprised that you remember, after all these years. You have repaid me poorly, after the efforts I have made, and the money I have expended, to ensure that you did not ruin yourself totally when you took it into your misguided head to play the actor instead of the soldier.'

'Forgive me, Father, that you find me in such straights, but I swear before God that they are not of my own making. I am the victim of a wicked apology for a man, who seeks to retain royal favour by accusing the innocent of things of which they are not guilty.'

'You speak of Cecil?' William enquired, and Oliver's eyes widened. 'You know?'

'I know Cecil, obviously,' William confirmed, 'and I was once proud to serve his father. But the apple has, it would seem, fallen far from the tree, and the son is not worthy of carrying the family name.'

'Neither, it would seem, am I,' Oliver muttered as he cast his eyes down over his filthy prison garb. William stood uncertainly for a moment, then a tear sprang to a corner of his eye as he recalled the eager-faced, cleanly scrubbed little boy who once rode proudly on the pommel of his saddle round and round the paddock on their modest estate in Middlesex. He choked it back, knelt and took Oliver's hand.

'If it be Cecil who accuses you, then I would rather believe your version of things,' he said kindly, and Oliver's tears ran freely down his grimy unshaven face as he grasped the proffered hand and began to explain.

'In truth, I was tricked into believing that what I did was in the nation's best interest,' he began. 'I admit that I wasted what might have been a worthy and prosperous career as a soldier, but I soon learned that I had not the stomach for the taking of life for no good reason. It was then that I joined a band of wandering players when I left the service of Essex in Ireland, as you are aware, and by this means did we become estranged.'

'I have ever blamed myself for that,' William confessed. 'I was still raw from the grief of your mother's passing, and could not accept that the gallant young man that we had raised together had, as it seemed to me, turned his back on an honourable life and taken to associating with vagabonds and prostitutes.'

'But you still sent me money to keep body and soul together,' Oliver reminded him, 'so you have no need to reproach yourself. I was lucky that the band with whom I associated knew their trade, and we now have a growing audience such that I feel that I may call myself an actor by profession. But Cecil took steps to expose me to a charge of desertion, when in fact I had secured an honourable discharge. He stooped low enough to steal my discharge paper, then threatened to voice it abroad that I was a deserter, thereby bringing about your public disgrace, and an end to your ambitions.'

'So you went along with his demands for my sake?' William enquired, and Oliver nodded. 'But with the completion of each task that was set me, it seemed that I was falling more and more into Cecil's net. After I identified a courier carrying messages to and from a man called William Walton in "The Clink", Cecil arranged for her to die in circumstances that implicated me, then when I met clandestinely with a renegade Jesuit called Gerard, he threatened to denounce me as a traitor. Finally I was prevailed upon to travel to York in order to obtain proof that a man named Sir George Brooke was involved in a plot to kidnap the King. I was able to identify and intercept a messenger passing between him and a certain Sir Griffin Markham with an estate in Nottinghamshire. From this messenger I learned not only that there was such a plot, but also its date.'

'The 24th June,' William muttered quietly, and Oliver looked up at him in surprise.

'You knew of that?' William nodded grimly.

'You are not the only one threatened by that oily lamprey Cecil. He visited me at Windsor, where I am currently Captain of the Guard, and all but demanded, as the price of your life, that I ride north and assassinate this messenger of whom you spoke. A man named Drysdale?'

'That is he, right enough,' Oliver confirmed. 'I am here precisely because I showed him mercy, once he had advised me of the date of the planned kidnap. By now he must have revealed to his master that their plot is revealed. What will you do?'

A broad smile crossed William's face as he sought confirmation of something Oliver had said a few moments earlier. 'You mentioned a man called George Brooke. He is a knight, and living in a clerical capacity in York?'

'Yes,' Oliver confirmed. 'I succeeded in gaining his confidence to such an extent that I was resident in his house for some days. It was by this means that I was able to identify the messenger passing between him and Markham, and I followed the man south and from him learned the date of the planned kidnap. Then in my stupidity I reported it to Cecil, who had me thrown in here because I had not killed the man. Now I would hazard a guess that he requires you to do so, if my life is to be spared. Why do you grin like that? Do you intend to carry out Cecil's evil request? I would not have you do that, even if it may mean that I remain in here.'

'I am smiling for two reasons,' William replied. 'The first is that despite all my foreboding, it would seem that I raised a son as honourably inclined as myself. The second is that you have revealed a weakness of Cecil's by means of which we may preserve both your life and our honour.'

'Can that devil have any weakness?' Oliver enquired hopefully, and William nodded.

'When you were at the house of Sir George Brooke, did he by any chance mention a brother? Or a sister?'

'No – why should he, and what significance does that hold?'

'George Brooke is the younger son of Baron Cobham, whose title passed to George's older brother Henry, and who

75

is now the Eleventh Baron of that title. Henry is currently in the Low Countries, where he is said to be close with the Count of Aremberg.'

'And what does this signify?' Oliver enquired somewhat testily, but the smile remained on his father's face as he continued to explain.

'The Count of Aremberg serves the House of Habsburg, which makes him open to the influence of the Spanish King Philip, and it is rumoured that he advises Philip in proposed negotiations for the peace treaty between England and Spain that our King James is so eager to promote. One of its proposed conditions, from the Spanish side, is greater tolerance for Catholics and their forms of worship.'

Oliver allowed all that to sink in before voicing how he summarised it. 'So the brother of George Brooke is in league with a man who is close to Philip of Spain, and who will be urging greater tolerance of Catholics here in England. What is so significant about that? We know that one brother – George, the man whose confidence I gained – was plotting to kidnap the King in order to bring this about, so why should it be such a revelation that his brother Henry is pursuing the same objective by means of his connection with the Spanish Court?'

'Their sister,' William replied with a broad smirk. 'What of her?' Oliver enquired, his thoughts almost swamped by all this detailed information.

'She was married to Cecil,' William advised him triumphantly, then watched as the son worked through this latest revelation.

'So Cecil is related by marriage to the very man that he had me spy upon? And this brother in the Low Countries who is possibly in league with Spain?'

'Yes and no,' William replied. 'Elizabeth Brooke was indeed married to Cecil the year after the defeat of the Armada, and by him she had a son called William. But she died some years ago now, so it is no longer strictly true that the brothers Brooke are his brothers in law.'

'But they once were?'

'Indeed they were, and who is to say that family loyalties do not still divert Cecil's hand? And for that matter, how would it bode for his ongoing power and position of trust in the Court of King James for his Majesty to be advised that one of Cecil's former brothers in law is implicated in a plot to kidnap the sovereign, while another is assisting the Spanish in the negotiations that are currently so dear to the King's heart?'

'You believe that we might divert Cecil's wrath by threatening to reveal his unfortunate choice of former wife?' Oliver enquired, but William shook his head.

'We go much deeper than that. Did Cecil say aught to you about apprehending George Brooke and bringing him south on a charge of treason?'

'No,' Oliver replied. 'But neither did he speak of proceeding against Markham. He was concerned only in securing the death of the messenger Drysdale.'

'And why might that be?' William prompted him. 'Think carefully, boy.' Suddenly Oliver got the point. 'Because he fears that his name might be mentioned once the family connection is revealed?'

'Precisely! If Brooke were to be dragged south and threatened with a traitor's death, would he not seek to use his family connection with Cecil to secure his freedom?'

'Indeed he might,' Oliver agreed. 'But Cecil would have him instantly silenced, would he not?'

'Undoubtedly,' William conceded. 'But his is not the only voice that might whisper uncomfortable truths in the King's ear.'

'The messenger Drysdale, you mean?' William sighed.

''Tis a pity you have not learned more from Cecil regarding the dirty ways in which these games are played,' William muttered. 'Drysdale will not live a day longer if Cecil gets his hands upon him, and how could he reveal a family connection of which he knows nothing?'

'So who, then?'

'Who else but the King's trusted Captain of the Windsor Guard?'

'You?'

'Yes, me. Cecil thought to play on my family loyalties in order to have his evil work conducted. I will play him at his own game. You will be released on my undertaking to hunt down the man Drysdale and put him to death. However, I will simply keep him close, but alive, while I travel north and secure Brooke. Once I have the brother in law in secure custody, and you are able to prove the connection between George Brooke and Sir Griffin Markham, we have Cecil firmly in the nutcrackers. Or perhaps, given where we currently sit, the thumbscrews might be a better analogy.'

'So I go north and seek the evidence against Markham?' Oliver enquired, and his father nodded.

'Indeed you do, which will of course necessitate your release. But Cecil will soon discover that he is not the only man capable of the foulest of blackmail. He should never have threatened the son with whom he has unwisely allowed me to become happily reconciled.'

Chapter Seven

'Pray silence for the return of the Prodigal Son,' Timothy Bryant muttered over the top of his ale mug as Oliver strode into the main room of The Cardinal with an awkward grin. 'Have you brought us that new comedy you've been promising us for months, or did you simply expect to walk back in here and take back all the leading parts?'

He seemed to be speaking for them all, to judge by the surly expressions around the table, and it was left to Meg Tyler to display some lingering affection for the man who had raised their company from nothing to where it currently was. 'We heard that you were in the Tower,' she said as she placed a cool hand on his tunic sleeve. 'Is that right?'

'Indeed I was,' Oliver confirmed, 'but while there I was able to complete the comedy of which Tim so kindly reminded me. It is all in my head, and all I require now is the time to commit it to written form.'

'The sooner the better,' Matthew Partridge grumbled. 'Our audiences get smaller by the day.'

'Did "The Maid of Orleans" not draw the crowds? Oliver enquired, somewhat at a loss to understand why, until Tim gave a sardonic guffaw. 'It seems that our audiences require only plays that involve Meg shedding some of her clothing. And, for preference, *all* of it.'

'So you would lose little by taking my saintly story on a tour of the nation?' Oliver enquired, relieved that he was not required to persuade his company to abandon a successful series of productions that enjoyed large and constant audiences.

'If they don't like it here in London, how might they be expected to like it elsewhere?' Meg enquired, and Oliver smiled. 'Because I have in mind presenting "The Maid of Orleans" in noble houses where they take their saints seriously.'

'You mean that I'll be able to do my death scene without the audience yelling for me to peel off my funeral gown?' Meg enquired eagerly, and Oliver nodded.

'Indeed, and in the house that I have in mind they would deem it blasphemy were you to do so.'

'They're Catholics, aren't they?' Tim enquired suspiciously, and Oliver nodded. 'Where else would we be likely to find such an appreciative assembly for whom to perform such a holy production?'

'And they will pay us?' Matthew Partridge enquired, and again Oliver nodded. 'Leave that to me. They will also feed us while we are among them, and I believe that once we have performed to satisfaction in one such house, there will be enthusiastic introductions to others.'

'Where do we begin?' was the next enquiry from another member of the company, and Oliver couldn't believe that it had been so easy.

'It just so happens that I have an introduction to a wealthy house in Nottinghamshire, where the knight who owns half the surrounding countryside is still grieving the loss of a beloved niece whose acquaintance I was fortunate to make recently. Prepare for travel, my fellow Thespians.'

***

William Wade was well ahead of his son as he announced his arrival to the seemingly indifferent gate guard at the only entrance to Nottingham Castle, a somewhat crumbling ruin of its former self. His name may have meant nothing to the guard on the gate, but his rank and office did, and within minutes he was drinking mulled claret with Governor Nicholas Mountjoy as they looked out over the grass-pocked parade ground, where a listless group of men at arms were being marched up and down by an officer whose voice was so loud that they could hear his yelled commands through the heavily mullioned glass of the front window.

'How go things at Windsor?' Mountjoy enquired. 'I must own that I yearn to return to a royal palace, where the action is constant and the living conditions far finer than in this draughty hovel.'

'You were once at Richmond, I believe?' William enquired out of politeness, and the ageing Nicholas nodded, then smiled as the memories returned.

'I was there for the glory days of her late Majesty, and well recall the comings and goings through the Gatehouse when Elizabeth went hunting in the Old Deer Park. Then I was offered this posting, and my wife was anxious to escape the unhealthy miasmas that drifted up from the river, so we came here, where the constant fogs took her life. Would that I had never left.'

'If it is any consolation,' Oliver advised him, 'our new King prefers Westminster, and when he wishes to hunt he comes out to Windsor, where we are kept on our mettle.'

'But why would the Captain of the Windsor Guard have business here in Nottingham?' William was asked, and he smiled. 'I wish to leave a prisoner here.'

'But you had no prisoner when you were admitted,' Mountjoy reminded him. 'Just two of your own men who rode with you.'

'This is true,' William conceded, 'but I had in mind the prisoner I shall be escorting upon my return. I believe that he may be found on an estate north of here, and Secretary Cecil is most anxious that he be detained for the safety of the realm.'

'A traitor, say you?'

'Indeed a traitor, in that he carried messages between one conspirator and another.'

'What nature of conspiracy would that be?' Mountjoy enquired, conscious of his isolation from London intrigue and gossip. 'Surely our new King has been well received?'

'By the majority, certainly,' William advised him, 'but there remain stubborn groups of Catholics who would that the throne had been bequeathed elsewhere.'

'We were advised that King James was Elizabeth's choice,' Mountjoy reminded him. 'Say you that we were deceived?'

'I remind you that we had only the word of Cecil that Elizabeth, on her death bed, passed the crown north of the border. And I refer of course to *Robert* Cecil, the son, not *William* Cecil the worthy statesman who was his father. And I have heard it whispered that Robert had long been in secret communication with James regarding the succession, and is now enjoying the fruits of his loyalty to an unknown ruler – one who is resented by those who were hoping for a return to Rome.' Mountjoy shuddered.

'My grandfather used to tell stories about the burnings during the reign of Mary – I freeze with terror simply by recalling his words. God forbid that those days should return. You may house your prisoner here, with my blessing. But is he not to be delivered on to London?'

'In good time, perhaps,' William advised him. 'But not until I can be certain that what he has to reveal will be made public knowledge, and not simply suppressed on the order of one man who might lose office by it.'

'Of whom do you speak?'

'I cannot say. In truth, I *dare* not say. But a man I would not trust with my life, or the safety of the nation. But ere I depart, I need directions to a place called Ollerton.'

***

Late that afternoon his horse seemed content to plod through scenery the like of which William had never before encountered. The York Road was hemmed in on either side by banks of silver birch, oaks, elms and chestnuts, and thick bracken sprang up between them to tumble carelessly onto the track that wound on ahead of him. It would a perfect place for an ambush, his soldier's training reminded him, and he recalled legends of a time when there were said to be outlaw bands roaming these parts. Even today there might be groups of footpads, men reduced by starvation to the robbery of innocent travellers who they had once defended as soldiers of a Queen who had abandoned them to grinding humiliating poverty once her immediate need of them had been eliminated by their efforts on her behalf.

There was a crossroads up ahead, and to one side of it an inn of some sort, and the lengthening shadows warned him that he would be risking life and limb to continue through a dark forest after nightfall, even though he was armed, trained to warfare, and accompanied by two seasoned members of his Windsor guard. He slid from his horse, handed its bridle to the bumbling halfwit who claimed to be the ostler, and walked inside seeking a bed for the night for himself and his two companions. Later, as his host presented him with a plate of greasy mutton chops and a mug of ale that tasted as if it had been watered down beyond any hope of flavour, William enquired as to his precise location.

'Yer in Edwinstowe,' the man advised him in a tone that suggested that his guest must be totally ignorant of the fame of his surroundings. William thanked him, and asked if he was on the right road to Ollerton. The innkeeper nodded.

'Straight on, less than 'alf a day's ride, master. Yer must be headed fer the Markham estate.'

'What makes you think that?' William enquired suspiciously, and the innkeeper took heed of the tone of voice. 'Didn't mean ter seem inquisitive or nothin', master – it's just that there's nowt in Ollerton but the Markham estate. Old Markham owns everything around them parts.'

'Do his retainers not have their own cottages?' William enquired. 'I'm in the King's service, and on most of the royal estates you may find outlying houses for his more menial attendants – those who don't live in the palaces themselves, that is.'

This had the desired effect on the very impressed innkeeper, who launched into a detailed explanation of who lived where for a twenty league radius of the inn from which he plied his trade. Obligingly, one reference was to a senior usher called Drysdale who was married to the landlord's sister in law, and who was sufficiently highly thought of by Sir Griffin Markham that Drysdale was able to bring trade to the inn at the crossroads in the form of travellers from the south who were heading for the estate.

'His wife – my sister in law – keeps bees in 'er garden,' the landlord added proudly as William pricked up his ears, 'and she sells the honey at the local market 'ere in Edwinstowe.'

Remembering that today was Friday, and with hope in his heart, William enquired as casually as he could 'When's your market day?'

'Tomorrow,' he was advised. 'They starts early, so after yer breakfast yer might want ter take a look afore yer journeys north. Just ask fer Mary Drysdale, and tell 'er that Edward Smout sent yer.'

The following morning William stifled the grumblings of his travelling companions regarding the uncomfortable night they had spent, and the quality of the food they had managed to exhort from the slovenly cook, with the glad tidings that if all went well they would be heading back to Nottingham Castle in time for the next sunset.

'We're bound for the local market,' William advised them. 'When we get there, the two of you lose yourselves in the trees that seem so abundant in these parts until you see me raise my bonnet, then hasten to my side with drawn swords. Any questions?'

There were none, and as the sun began to climb above the tree line William sauntered up to a stall on the village green, behind which a portly middle-aged lady was standing proudly behind earthenware jars of different sizes that had already secured the attention of swarms of flies, to judge by her constant waving of hands and irritated mutters. Behind her, a man of approximately her own age was unloading more jars and placing them carefully on the grass behind the stall.

'Mistress Drysdale?' William enquired innocently, and the woman nodded. 'That's me – Mary Drysdale. Yer lookin' fer some of the best honey south o' Doncaster? A penny a small jar, penny ha'penny the big uns. Robbie, show the man one o' them big uns fresh from the wagon.'

Secure in the belief that he had the right man, William raised his bonnet, and the man and wife behind the stall looked on, wide-eyed with fear, as two men ran up to William's side with drawn swords. William smiled reassuring at their quarry.

'Robert Drysdale, you have nothing to fear if you come along with us without resistance. My name is William Wade, and I arrest you in the name of King James on an accusation of high treason. Should you show any sign of resistance, your life is forfeit – otherwise, you may rely on being gently handled as we travel south.'

Drysdale was led away, his face a picture of abject terror, while his wife simply stared after him with an open mouth. William extracted a twopenny coin from his purse and laid it down gently on the trestle table as he smiled at her reassuringly and lifted one of the large earthenware jars.

'He will come to no harm, but he may be gone for some time. At least you sold some of your honey, and you may keep the change.'

Back in Nottingham, William assisted Drysdale down from the neck of the horse on which he had spent an uncomfortable day's ride south to Nottingham, and kept hold of him by the wrist, prior to handing him over to one of his escort. 'Take him to the Gaol Keeper, and tell him that he is to be treated kindly, else the man will answer to me.'

'Thank God we're back in civilisation,' the other escort muttered as he stretched his legs and gazed out beyond the Castle walls into the lanes that led to the first of the town houses. 'Indeed, but not for long,' William advised him.

'Tomorrow you and Ralph may head back to London with a message for my son that it is safe for a band of wandering players to approach the Markham estate, then you may resume your duties at Windsor.'

'You will not be travelling with us, sir?'

'No, indeed not,' William smiled. 'Tomorrow I shall head back north, to York, there to secure custody of a far more important piece on the chessboard of this current treason. However, I shall avoid staying at a certain inn at Edwinstowe, where the landlord would be likely to piss in my ale in revenge for the arrest of his brother in law.'

***

'Do not offer me your mealy-mouthed excuses, Cecil,' James requested in a voice dripping in warning, 'else I shall be obliged to conclude that I chose ill when I placed the safety of my new kingdom in your hands. Are there plots against my throne, or are there not?'

'There are none, Your Majesty,' Cecil hastened to assure him. 'There was one, but it was suppressed ere it could become anything other than a matter for idle discussion among little men with more ambition than followers.'

'On the subject of little men,' James replied with a cruel smirk, 'what provision have you made for my security at Windsor? I journey there in a week's time, yet when I sent my Chamberlain hence to discuss household arrangements with the Captain of the Windsor Guard, he was informed that the man was missing without reason. Was he one of those who was plotting against me?'

Cecil was obliged to think quickly. On the one hand, he could not afford to allow James to think for one moment that he was unable to explain the absence of such an important link in the chain of royal security, but on the other hand he could not explain that he had ordered William Wade to journey north in search of a messenger travelling between two conspirators who, or so he had just informed the King, no longer existed. He opted for what he hoped would be a non-committal response.

'The man is taking some leave with his family, Your Majesty.' James looked down at him through eyes hooded in disbelief. 'Surely, were that the case, this fact would have been known to his deputy, to whom my Chamberlain spoke, and who claimed to have no knowledge of the man's whereabouts.'

'There has clearly been a simple failure in communication, Your Majesty, and I will look into the matter immediately. But you have my assurance that it will be safe for you to journey to Windsor as planned.'

'See that it is, Cecil, because if you are simply offering me your assurance that there are no plots against me in order to retain your favoured status, it will go the worse for you. You may withdraw.'

Cecil all but flew down the stairs that divided the Royal Suite from his more humble accommodation on the lower level, and sent a messenger with an urgent summons to the Lieutenant of the Tower. As the man stood apprehensively before him an hour later, twisting his bonnet nervously in front of him, Cecil chose to remain seated so as not to emphasise the difference in height between them as he pierced the man with an angry glare.

'You recently released a man named Oliver Wade?'

'Yes indeed, my Lord, on your order.'

'Regardless of that, the release order was in your name?'

'Naturally, my Lord, since that is the correct procedure.'

'Regardless of any of that, you may be held responsible should he prove to be of danger to the throne, may you not?'

'Only if you were to deny having issued the order, my Lord.'

'An order that was not in writing?'

'Indeed not, such is my trust in your Lordship's honour and integrity.'

'You should trust no man in these uncertain times,' Cecil smirked back at the man, who was clearly terrified. 'However, there is one way in which you may retrieve your good name and retain your position.'

'What is that, my Lord?'

'I wish you to send a large contingent of men to the estate of Sir Griffin Markham in North Nottinghamshire. They are to bring back everyone they find there. One of them will be the suspected traitor Oliver Wade. I want them all in the Tower by the end of next week.'

The Lieutenant hurried out, and Cecil sighed with satisfaction. Once Oliver Wade was back in the Tower on more false charges, the father would come to heel, hopefully having killed Markham's messenger. Then Cecil could see to what would hopefully appear to be the seemingly pointless murder of Brooke, before he could go telling tales that were best left untold.

Chapter Eight

'You met with my niece?' Sir Griffin Markham enquired with a watering eye as Oliver stood before him in the drawing room of the manor house on the Markham estate, while the remaining members of his company rested outside on the sloping front lawn, glad to have finished the journey that had taken almost two footsore weeks in indifferent weather.

'Indeed I did,' Oliver replied huskily with a faked tear of his own. 'She was the most beautiful woman I ever laid eyes on, and would that our respective ranks had been other than they were. As it was, I was fortunate to be of service to her as she made her way from one of her weekly visits to your friend in somewhat reduced circumstances in Southwark. She was set upon by footpads, who I chased off, and she very kindly entertained me to supper at her inn. I was due to accompany her on her next visit, but was cruelly robbed of that opportunity to become better acquainted with her by an explosion at that same inn, the cause of which remains a mystery to this day.'

'So why are you here now, along with that ragged band outside?' Markwell queried, and Oliver feigned a shamefaced look as he replied. 'You must forgive my impertinence in journeying here with my fellow actors, but I was led to believe, during my all too brief acquaintance with the beautiful Lady Harriet, that you might welcome the diversion of a play devoted to one of the saints revered by the Church that the former Queen sought to suppress without any regard for the welfare of her soul.'

'You are of the Catholic faith?' Sir Griffin enquired with a look of surprise mingled with suspicion, and Oliver allowed his gaze to sink to the floor.

'Forgive me, my Lord, but it would not be safe for either of us were I to declare my religious beliefs on our first acquaintance. However, regardless of any fear of persecution, there can surely be no offence in devoting my life to recreating, for the education and diversion of those who truly worship God, the lives of our worthy saints. It was in the belief that it would have gladdened the heart of that beautiful woman whose death we both mourn were I to present one of these dramatic works to yourself and your household that I have walked here along with my fellow performers in order to do so. Even should that not be your wish, perhaps out of Christian charity you might offer some simple refreshment ahead of our departure, with perhaps some indication of where we might find another estate upon which our humble offerings might be more acceptable.'

He suppressed a grin of triumph as Sir Griffin replied eagerly that he would be more than happy to accommodate the players for several days, in order that they might perform their play in memory of the tragically doomed Lady Harriet. He gave orders that the grooms' quarters above the stables, which were currently unoccupied, were to be made ready to receive the remainder of the company. 'Since the tragic death of my niece I have no longer required a coach, since I rarely travel outside the estate,' Sir Griffin explained, 'and for the same reason I now employ only two grooms for my modest collection of horses, and they can be allocated pallets in the stables themselves.'

'At least it's better than the hedge bottoms we've been

sleeping in,' Matthew Partridge observed as Oliver walked out onto the front lawn to smilingly advise the company that 'We go on in two evenings' time, in the Great Hall.'

'I hope that I'll be afforded a degree of privacy,' Meg Tyler responded, to a chortle from several of the male actors. When she raised her eyebrows questioningly, it was Jamie Winters who spoke for the rest when he reminded her that 'There's not much of you that we haven't seen daily anyway,' to which she retorted hotly 'Well, you ain't seen *that* bit, and you're not going to.'

The whole of the next two days was taken up in rehearsing the play that had already been staged to lacklustre audiences back in Shoreditch, with Oliver undertaking the role of Chorus. He was pleasantly surprised by the grace and simplicity with which Meg carried off the role of the pious country girl who became God's warrior for the Dauphin, ably portrayed in his youthful enthusiasm by Matthew Partridge. They rapidly became friendly with the Cook, and were kept almost continually fed with pastries and small beer as they rehearsed enthusiastically in the rear courtyard, and Oliver had almost forgotten the real reason why they were there until he noticed, on the second day of their rehearsals, the steady arrival on foot of pale-faced young men dressed in simple garments who were admitted through a side door to the main house by the Steward to the estate, who never once appeared to enquire as to their identity.

Convinced in his own mind that these mysterious arrivals were Catholic priests, and that Cecil would be more than grateful to learn of the welcome they were receiving from Markham, Oliver began making plans to somehow get a message back to his father, assuming that he was back in

Windsor, having succeeded in securing the messenger Drysdale, and perhaps even Sir George Brooke. But unless he could commandeer a horse, whoever went south with this importance intelligence – and he did not rule out himself, given that the Chorus role in the upcoming play could easily be taken over by Tim Bryant while doubling as the Pope – it would be a long, weary and hazardous journey back south. Then the evening of the performance arrived all too soon, and Oliver was obliged to concentrate his attention on the play.

The company had been fed earlier that day by the obliging Cook, and were therefore not distracted by the delicious smells drifting from the several large tables to the side of the Great Hall nearest to the brick fireplace and chimney as they organised the area on the other side that had been allocated to them as their performing space. It was not a raised stage, and they would therefore need to come closer to their audience in order to be seen and heard, but this did not dishearten them as the usual nervousness set in ahead of a performance. The door leading to the stairs that served the basement kitchen had been left ajar, and they had been allowed to hang an old curtain in the opening so that they could enter and leave the stage area. When a costume change was required – and particularly for Meg, who was required to don at least three costumes during the one hour for which the production ran – the actors could hide behind a screen at the top of the kitchen stairs, and the various items that they needed to carry on stage, such as the Pope's crozier and Joan's simple cross, were laid out on a table just behind the curtain.

Inside the Hall, candles had been lit in all the holders suspended from the ceiling, and the log fire was crackling merrily, as Oliver stepped from behind the curtain in the gold floor length robe that the Chorus always wore regardless of the production, and delivered his opening lines with a beaming smile. It fell silent along the trestles loaded with food, and it did not escape his attention that at least half the audience crossed themselves as the performance began, almost as if they were warding off the Devil. Then as Oliver walked off, he was replaced on stage by Meg, dressed in a simple country girl's smock and carrying the stool on which she sat in order to receive the visitation from St Michael.

One by one the actors performed their roles with a skill and fluency that had never been possible while being heckled by half-drunken oafs who'd paid their penny to enter the undercroft of The Cardinal back in Shoreditch, and were determined to see something bawdy. The entire production came to its climax as 'The Maid' made her last obeisance to God, while two of the remaining cast symbolically lifted a red blanket from the floor to depict the rising flames. With a final shriek to God to receive her soul Meg finished her soliloquy, and total silence ensued, followed five seconds later by rapturous shouts of appreciation and much clapping of hands.

The entire company reassembled in front of what had been a funeral pyre only seconds previously, and took several bows before the audience ran out of energy for applause. Sir Griffin Markham smilingly beckoned Oliver forward, and handed him a soft bag heavy with coin, inviting his company to remain in order to give a return performance the following evening. After sinking copious quantities of small beer and chewing through a welcome late supper of leftovers from the main banquet, they divided the money between themselves and sank thankfully onto their pallets above the stables after one of the best audience receptions they could ever remember.

It was barely light before they came awake again to the sound of raised voices, the tramping of heavy boots and the stomping up the wooden staircase that preceded a loud command for them all to get to their feet without delay or resistance.

Oliver roused himself and climbed out of his bedding as commanded, to the sight of half a dozen heavily armed men. 'Outside, all of you,' their leader demanded.

'For what reason?' Oliver enquired, and the man glared at him. 'Because I say so, shit-face, and I come on the orders of the King. Everyone we find here is to be taken under escort to Nottingham Castle, there to await transport to London on charges of treason.'

Oliver laughed, if only to reassure the rest of his company, whose terror was written clearly in their faces. 'We are a mere company of theatrical players who were commissioned to perform for the entertainment of Sir Griffin Markham and his friends. How can that be deemed treason?'

'I do not intend to argue with you, big mouth, since my orders are to apprehend everyone found here. Quite a collection, as it transpires – there must be thirty or so downstairs, already waiting to depart. So cease your noise and get down there and join them!'

Oliver was in the process of grudgingly obeying the command when he became aware of a commotion at the far end of the stable loft that they were all occupying. A section had been screened off with cloaks in order to provide Meg Tyler with some primitive privacy, and one of the armed intruders had pulled the cloaks down with the tip of his sword in order to investigate what lay beyond. A startled Meg Tyler had leapt from her bedding clad only in a shift that barely covered her knees, voicing an outraged protest, and the ruffian had stepped forward to grab her with one arm, then dropped his sword to the boards in order to paw her body roughly with his other hand.

Meg was howling her indignant protests when Oliver rushed to the far end of the loft, picked up the sword and threatened to run the man through if he did not unhand her. Then he felt a heavy blow to the back of his head, and everything went blank.

He came round slowly to several sensations at once. His head was throbbing fiercely, and there was a bright light in his face. Underneath him he was conscious of a lurching and swaying sensation that sent an ache through every bone in his body, but the one consolation appeared to be that his head was resting on something soft and squishy. He opened his eyes cautiously, but all that met his gaze was a blinding blue sky, and he quickly closed them again before he heard a soft voice somewhere above his head. 'Thank God you're still alive', it said, and he reopened his eyes and looked carefully to his right, into the tear-streaked face of Meg Tyler, whose ample bosom was obviously the soft cushion on which his head was lying.

'Where in Hell are we?' he enquired groggily. 'On our way to Nottingham, according to that arsehole who seems to be in charge,' Meg advised him, before leaning down and kissing him warmly on the lips. 'Thank you for what you did – you're a true gentleman, and I owe you what little honour I still have left.'

'Honour or not, you have the makings of a fine actress,' Oliver assured her as he tried to stretch out his legs, but felt only a bony resistance, and heard a shout of protest from Tim Bryant. 'I may not be such a gifted performer as the lady whose titties you're using as a cushion, but there's no need to boot my arse!'

Oliver apologised, then levered himself upright with the aid of a panel of wood that proved to be the side of a wagon as it rumbled along a dusty track surrounded on either side by trees and lower vegetation. A swift look to the front and the rear revealed that the wagon that seemed dangerously overburdened with his entire company sprawled uncomfortably along its length was only one in a long caravan of wagons, each being pulled by either a horse or an ox, and with armed men on horseback interspersed between them. The blinding sun lay to their left, from which Oliver deduced that they were travelling south at sometime ahead of noon. His memory of the town of Nottingham through which they had travelled almost a week ago was that it lay almost a day's ride south of the Markham estate, and it was to be hoped that it would not be long before this miserable jolting journey came to a merciful end.

Two hours later it did, although they had been able to relieve the boredom for a full hour prior to that, as they watched the crenulated battlements of its ancient Castle perched high on its sandstone base becoming larger and larger before they passed the first of the outlying cottages. They trundled into a sloping area immediately inside the entrance gate, and the commander shouted loudly for the procession to come to a halt. Then they were all ordered out of the wagons, to stand in a line.

Two men in rich clothing walked down from the Castle itself, and with a lurch of joy Oliver recognised one of them as his father. Rather than shout out, and invite a smack in the head from a sword hilt, he waited until the leader of their escort saluted the other man smartly and announced that he had a large body of prisoners to be housed in the cells below the Castle ahead of their being sorted out, then led down to London to await their fates. Oliver watched as his father casually surveyed the ragged collection of prisoners, then stopped, wide -eyed, when his glance came to rest on him.

'Where did you acquire these prisoners, pray?' he enquired with a broad smile.

'Up north, Captain,' the man replied, clearly aware of William Wade's true identity. 'What brings *you* north, pray?' he added by way of casual enquiry. 'Mind your own business,' William replied curtly, 'but how much care did you take to ascertain the identities of those you seized?'

'Very little was needed, sir, since we were ordered to bring in anyone we found on the Markham estate. That's Markham himself, in the blue tunic, looking slightly better dressed than the rest of them. But half of them would seem to be Catholic priests, so Cecil will no doubt reward us handsomely.'

'And I will reward you with a week in the very cells that you seem happy to be about to fill if you do not release my son immediately,' William growled, to a look of astonishment from both the leader of the incoming escort and the Governor of the Castle. William walked over to Oliver with a broad smile and embraced him warmly, causing him to wince.

'Has one of these oafs injured you?' he enquired solicitously, but Oliver shook his head, then winced again as he wished he hadn't. 'A blow to the head only, Father, but a good one, probably delivered with a sword hilt.'

'Well,' William smiled, much relieved, 'it seems that once again you require your father to come to your rescue. Are those by whom you are surrounded all part of your acting company?'

'Indeed they are,' Oliver confirmed proudly, calling them out one by one to stand a few paces ahead of the rest of the prisoners. Meg gave a slight curtsy as she stepped a few paces forward, and William grinned. 'I thought that women were not allowed to perform in the theatre. Or does she fulfil some other role in your life?' Oliver looked slightly shocked.

'She is indeed a fine actress, and we defy convention by presenting her to audiences.'

'And I shall defy convention by having you all released without charge,' William grinned. 'Apart from my rank, the man who brought you back here from Markham has learned more than once, while serving under me at Westminster some years ago, that I can be unforgiving if disobeyed. Gather the rest of your company, and present them to the Palace Cook. She's an old soak, but they look as if they could gratefully consume anything she prepares for them. The prisoners will no doubt tell Cecil all he wants to know, and he will no doubt be more than anxious to take the credit, allowing us to return to our regular callings. As for you, join me in the Governor's residence and let's drink to our continuing reunion. But the next time we meet by accident, please contrive not to be someone's prisoner.'

Chapter Nine

'So how much did you get out of Markham?' William enquired of Oliver as they sat side by side in the morning room, on the banque by the window that overlooked the private castle garden, drinking mulled wine and enjoying the pleasant aroma from the pine log fire.

'Nothing, apart from the fact that I believe that he harbours Catholic priests,' Oliver replied gloomily. 'We weren't there long enough for me to acquire his confidence, but I think that half the men apprehended when the King sent that lot after us will prove to be Jesuits, so that should be enough to ensure Markham's trial for treason, should it not?'

'His death, more likely,' William grimaced. 'Those men were sent by Cecil, and I doubt that the King knows anything about it. I'm sure Cecil wants to despatch anyone who can prove his link to his former brother in law Brooke.'

'Where is Brooke now?' Oliver enquired. 'Did you manage to bring him down to Nottingham?'

'I did indeed, with a little assistance from the garrison at York, who have all now gone back north. You probably passed them on your way down here.'

'And is Brooke secure in the cells beneath here?'

'He certainly is, although all he seemed prepared to tell me was that he was Cecil's brother in law, and that I would sincerely regret laying hands on him and accusing him of matters of which he was innocent.'

'So he hasn't confessed to any involvement with Markham, or any plot to kidnap the King?'

'No. He went so far as to deny knowing Drysdale, even when I confronted the two of them with each other. Drysdale just looked terrified, while Brooke demanded to know who the man was, and what possible connection he might have with a man who looked like a peasant off the land.'

'You obviously didn't kill Drysdale, as Cecil instructed?'

'Of course not. If put to the question, I feel sure that the man will obligingly reveal that he acted as a messenger between Brooke and Markham, and that both men knew of a plot to kidnap the King on 24th June. A plot that must surely now have come to nothing, since we have the main conspirators in irons.'

'But how do we know that?' Oliver enquired. 'There could be others, and they may strike at the King in order to secure the release of Markham and Brooke. If that happens, Cecil will fall from grace, and his wrath will be both terrible and merciless.' William smiled.

'You forget that should that eventuate, Cecil will no longer wield the power that he does at present. Nor will he, in all likelihood, should his links through marriage with the Brooke family become known to the King. But I fear that Cecil will have George Brooke quietly done to death well before that happens, which is why I am keeping him safely guarded down below, with two of the Governor's most trusted men responsible for his continued life.'

'If he remains alive,' Oliver mused as an idea began to form in his head, 'will he not seek to plead his relationship with Cecil in order to escape death as a traitor?'

'Of course he will,' William confirmed, 'which is the very reason why Cecil will have him quietly murdered once he is in the Tower.'

'But you spoke of another brother, did you not?' Oliver reminded him. 'One who advises the Spanish King? If that comes to the knowledge of the King, will he not stay Cecil's hand, in case it goes ill for his ambition to make peace with Philip of Spain?'

'He certainly will, if that connection is revealed to King James. But if Brooke is dead before that happens, how can that come about?'

'Suppose Brooke were to put it all in writing while he remains here in Nottingham?'

William laughed out loud. 'He trusts me even less than he probably now trusts you, so how could he be persuaded that such a document would be in his best interests to compile?'

'What makes you think that he does not trust me?' Oliver enquired with a slow smile. 'May I assume that Brooke and Drysdale have not spoken since you brought them both down here?'

'Of course they haven't, as I already advised you. They stood face to face, and each denied knowledge of the other.'

'And they remain separately confined?'

'Indeed, but so what?'

'The "so what", Father, is that Drysdale has had no occasion to advise Brooke of my true identity, and the fact that at sword point I forced him to disclose details of the kidnap plot.'

'Again, your drift?'

'Brooke still knows me as the eager writer of mystery plays – the secret Catholic who prevailed upon his hospitality in York. His housekeeper caught me looking through documents in his study, and no doubt lost little time in advising him of that, but supposing that I pretend that this was because I was suspicious that Drysdale might have left explosives in the house?'

'I cannot for the life of me understand what it is that you propose,' his father complained as he stared hard into his face. 'Do you plan to ease yourself back into Brooke's confidence?'

'And why should I not?' Oliver enquired eagerly. 'If you were to throw me in the same cell as him, accusing me of being discovered in Markham's house when the King's men arrived, I can then worm my way back into his confidence by pretending that I was in Markham's service all along, and that Drysdale was no longer trusted. I might even go so far as to insinuate that Brooke had been given the wrong date for the kidnapping.'

William's mouth fell open in admiration. 'I'm not sure whether it's to your credit or not, but you seem to have acquired the same capacity for underhanded double-dealing as Cecil himself.'

'I was well taught, of course,' Oliver reminded him, 'but to that I can add my playwright's skill. He who is capable of inventing stories to entertain the mob is also capable of composing intricate deceptions. Added to which, I can carry it all off with an actor's talent for appearing to be that which he is not, as Cecil once described it.'

'And once you have Brooke's confidence, what do you propose?'

'That I persuade him to let me assist in the drafting of a document that will go under his hand, in which he pleads kinship with Cecil and denies all knowledge of any plot to kidnap the King. He will believe that this will save his neck, as indeed it might, if Cecil wishes to keep their relationship from the King's ears.'

'And if Cecil simply has Brooke done to death?'

'Then at the very least we have a document under Brooke's hand that Cecil will pay dearly to have suppressed. It should prove sufficient for you and I to slide out from under his slimy grip. You return to Windsor with your reputation intact, and I return to my theatre.'

William remained so deep in thought that Oliver was searching in his mind for some flaw that he had overlooked, but eventually his father looked up with a smile.

'You seem to crave suffering, but let us at least try out your plan. If it comes to nought, then we ourselves have lost nothing. Except several days of comfort for you, of course.'

'If this plan works,' Oliver grinned back, 'it will have been worth it.'

Three days later the door to the cell that Oliver had been sharing with Brooke was pulled noisily open, and a jailor grabbed Oliver by the scruff of his heavily soiled tunic and dragged him into the corridor, slamming the door behind him after yelling loudly that 'You're wanted upstairs, scum! God help you when the Governor is advised of your true identity!'

'Hopes I didn't overdo it just then,' the jailor muttered once they were out of earshot of the cell, and he attempted to dust down Oliver's tunic. 'Far from it,' his pretended prisoner advised him with a grin, 'but lose no time in taking me back to my father, and hopefully a decent dinner.'

The broad grin on Oliver's face said it all as William hurried into the Great Hall, and his son looked up from the dinner table at which he sat alone, wiping turkey crumbs from his mouth with a napkin.

'I hope that the smirk that wreaths your countenance bodes well for our enterprise,' William remarked as he helped himself to a mug of wine before taking a seat, extracting his eating knife and carving himself a slice of pork. Oliver's grin remained where he had left it as he reached inside his doublet pocket and extracted three folded pages of vellum.

'You are about to reap the rewards of employing that very expensive tutor who taught me my letters,' he smirked as he laid the pages on the table in front of William on the opposite side. His father glanced down at it briefly, then invited Oliver to give him 'the gist of what the man had to impart'.

'Put simply,' Oliver advised him triumphantly, 'he admits to knowing Markham, indeed to having been a friend of his for some years. Then he goes on to insist that out of loyalty for his former brother in law Cecil, for whom he retains the highest respect and regard, he only pretended to become involved in Markham's scheme to kidnap the King, along with several other minor nobles that he names. It is all in my hand, but with Brooke's at the foot thereof.'

'So he confirms the existence of the plot, and Markham's part in it?'

'Indeed he does, but there is more, on which I require your wise counsel.'

'And this is?'

'The other brother, Henry – the one who currently enjoys the family title of Lord Cobham.'

'What of him?'

'According to Brooke, his older brother is involved in more than simply a plot to bring pressure on King James, and even more than kidnapping him.'

'He plans to assassinate him?' William demanded, awe-stricken by what he was hearing. 'Probably,' Oliver replied, 'since it is the ultimate ambition of this Henry Brooke and his associates to replace King James on his throne by someone of purer Tudor blood.'

'There are none, surely?' William queried, and Oliver shrugged his shoulders. 'I know not, but if so, then clearly there is a much deeper plot of which even Cecil is probably unaware.'

'Before we return officially to London,' William replied, 'I will journey to Windsor and have this document safely secured in the vaults there. Then I will rejoin you and the rest of what will no doubt be a lengthy progress into London and direct to the Tower. If I adjudge aright, Cecil will be waiting in order to arrest us; me for deserting my post, and you for being in the company of a conspirator against the King, not to mention a cartload of Catholic priests.'

'He really is the Devil incarnate, is he not?' Oliver shuddered, but the smile had not left his father's face. 'In your plays, does the Devil not always get his just desserts? It's time for that fox Cecil to learn that sometimes the chickens in the henhouse can prove too dangerous to take on.'

'A worthy haul,' Cecil smiled with satisfaction as he sat with Oliver and William in the private quarters of the Lieutenant of the Tower, who had tactfully withdrawn about his routine business. 'We have Markham and Brooke falling over themselves, each eager to cast the blame wholly on the other. Their confessions will not need to be forced, since they are volunteered. In addition, we have a fine collection of Jesuit priests who we can either burn in the old tradition, or draw and quarter, with their heads displayed in a neat row on London Bridge.'

'No-one could accuse you of not enjoying your work,' William observed sardonically, 'but may we both assume that you are finished with us, for the time being at least?'

'Provided that you say nothing of the depth of your involvement in all this,' Cecil replied with some reluctance. 'I wish to be in a position to advise His Majesty merely that all this was brought about by agents working for me, without disclosing their identities. This will of course conform to the need for secrecy and discretion in such matters.'

'And then there would be no risk of anyone reminding His Majesty of how close one of the conspirators may be linked to the man in whom he places so much trust?' William enquired ominously, and Cecil's face darkened.

'To what do you refer?' he enquired. 'It is true that in a moment of weakness many years in the past, I took a wife, mainly on the insistence of the late Queen. It is also true that at the time, the Brooke family were highly regarded, to the extent that Elizabeth had offered George higher preferments. These were unfortunately not forthcoming before her tragic death, and our current King has not seen fit to honour them. This is no doubt why George was so easily misled by others, but during all the years that I was married to his sister, there was never a breath of suspicion regarding George Brooke's loyalty to the crown.'

'And the other brother?' Oliver enquired with an engaging smile.

'Of which brother do you speak?' Cecil enquired as the colour drained from his face.

'Henry Brooke, Lord Cobham, currently located in the Low Countries, and said to have the ear of King Philip of Spain,' Oliver replied with a confident smile. 'You surely cannot have forgotten that you had more than one brother in law. And how loyal is Henry to King James's cause?'

'I know nought of his loyalty,' Cecil replied evasively.

'Because there is none,' William muttered ominously. 'We have intelligence that he plans to replace James with another who is of purer Tudor blood.'

Cecil's look of terror was almost certainly not feigned, as he looked desperately from father to son, his head closely resembling a tennis ball passing back and forth in the royal courts at Hampton Court Palace. 'How can you know of this?' he croaked, and it was Oliver's turn to look smug.

'You under-estimated my skill as a spy, Sir Robert,' he goaded him. 'And you under-estimated the guilt that weighs upon Sir George Brooke's soul. He confessed all to me while we were imprisoned together. On your orders, you will recall – you instructed those you sent to Markham to imprison everyone they found there. I was one of many, and due to a shortage of cells at Nottingham Castle we were cooped up more than one to a cell. George Brooke still trusted me, as the result of more of your deviousness, and he confessed all to me. I have it in writing under his hand.'

'You must hand over that document!' Cecil demanded, to hoots of laughter from father and son. It was William who supplied their answer.

'It is securely locked in a place where you cannot access it, Sir Robert. May we now leave, with no remaining blemish on our reputations?'

'You will not prove your loyalty to King James by flushing out those who would seek to replace him?' Cecil all but pleaded. Oliver turned and smiled as the two men headed for the chamber door.

'My father must resume his duties at Windsor, before you have him decried as a deserter. And I have a comedy that I am long overdue writing. I wish I could commission a portrait of your countenance as it is at present, for I would gladly employ it as my muse.'

Endnote

Dear Reader,

Thank you for joining me in this unsettled period of England's history, and I hope you enjoyed your time there. Surprisingly, most of the story you have just read was based on historical fact. While Oliver Wade and his company of actors were fictitious, the remaining characters – including William Wade - are drawn straight from recorded history, and the main events depicted really occurred.

During her last few days of life, the dying Elizabeth 1st was largely comatose, silent and somewhat delusional. Apart from her loyal Ladies, the only one consistently by her death bed was her Secretary of State, Sir Robert Cecil, pleading with her to at long last name her successor. He emerged from her death chamber with the tidings that when he had mentioned James VI of Scotland, the son of the executed Mary Queen of Scots, Elizabeth had smiled and raised one finger in order to describe a circlet above her head, which Cecil interpreted as a gesture of consent. Why she had not simply nodded remained unexplained.

There was no-one who could corroborate what Cecil had alleged, but he lost no time in proclaiming that England had a new King, to be crowned as James 1st, employing a form of words he had prepared in advance. He had in fact been in secret communication with James for some time prior to that, and entertained high hopes that he would continue as the trusted right-hand man behind the throne.

But he rapidly learned that this was to be a new form of

monarchy, since James had very firm views on kingship. Whereas 'Gloriana' had relied on public adulation, James had been tutored, during his early years ruling under regents, to believe that monarchs were appointed by God, and ruled by divine right. He was to pass these views on to his heir Charles 1ˢᵗ, with tragic consequences, but for the time being Cecil was required to rule the nation in all but name, leaving James to issue the orders without reference to anyone else, not even his own Council, and certainly not a Parliament full of commoners.

One of the flies in the royal ointment that Cecil was required to remove was the ongoing demand by groups of noble Catholics for greater religious freedom. James was a lifelong Protestant, and was not about to pay homage to the Pope. When this became obvious, various plots took form, the first of which is the central theme of this novel – the plan to kidnap the King and hold him to ransom for enhanced tolerance of the old religion. This conspiracy has become known to historians as the 'Bye Plot', since it existed inside a larger one known as the 'Main Plot', that envisaged the removal of James from the throne entirely, to be replaced by a cousin of sorts, Arabella Stuart. This will be the central core of the second novella in the series, 'All for Arabella'.

But the ultimate planned treachery was the far better remembered 'Gunpowder Plot', and its scapegoat Guy Fawkes, whose effigy is still ceremonially burned on bonfires around the world even today. The objective of this conspiracy was to blow James, his Council and most of his immediate family, into oblivion during the State Opening of Parliament in November 1605. A positive banquet for historical novelists such as myself, and Oliver Wade's part in thwarting this evil scheme forms the third and final novella in the series.

I'd be delighted to hear from you, either indirectly by way of a book review on Amazon or 'Goodreads', or more intimately either on Twitter, or through my Facebook website **davidfieldauthor**.

David

*

Printed in Poland
by Amazon Fulfillment
Poland Sp. z o.o., Wrocław